D1738931

THE
New Austerities

ℚ
PUBLISHED BY
Peachtree Publishers, Ltd.
494 Armour Circle, NE
Atlanta, Georgia 30324

Jacket design by Loraine Balcsik and
            Nicola Simmonds Carter
Interior design by Jennifer Knight
Jacket photograph, "Windows at Chapel of Ease," 1988,
            © Karekin Goekjian

Manufactured in the United States of America

10 9 8 7 6 5 4 3 2 1

Library of Congress Cataloging-in-Publication Data

Perdue, Tito.
            The new austerities / Tito Perdue.
                        p. cm.
            ISBN 1-56145-086-3
            1. United States—Social life and customs—
Fiction. 2. Married people—Travel—East (U.S.)—Fiction.
3. Marriage—United States—Fiction. 4. Men—United
States—Fiction. I. Title.
PS3566.E691225N48 1994   93-49795
813' .54—dc20   CIP

T H E

New Austerities

TITO

PERDUE

PEACHTREE
PUBLISHERS

In latter days, with time winding down,
he used to rise up after each
ten thousand years and offer praises
to the sun. Now, lifting both arms,
once more he pronounced the old phrases,
and then sent them off on their long journey
through nights and days.

He was in a city,
to judge by many things: smoke rising from
the avenues, and flat clay roofs as far as
eye could see. "Hmmm," said he, nodding wisely.
"Sumer this is, famous for its honey.
Yea, and Akkad for the bees!" And that, of course,
was when an airplane crossed overhead.
Too amazed to scream, he leapt to the balustrade
(but why was he naked?) and stood gazing
down into the late modern crevices of a city
more familiar to him than his own.

PART

I

Chapter One

TO NORTH WAS FOG, SOUTH SMOKE; IT WAS WHEN HE TURNED AND
FACED INTO THE VAST GREY BUILDING TO THE WEST THAT HE SAW HOW
EACH SEPARATE WINDOW LOOKED IN UPON EACH NEW LATE-TWENTIETH-
CENTURY OCCUPATION, SEQUENTIALLY ARRANGED. Someone, he saw,
was at a computer, while someone else (his feet were sticking
out) had gotten beneath the machine itself, apparently to
make a repair. For the most part however his attention came
to rest upon a tall woman who was so stiff, so rectitudinous-
looking and so constrained, she might almost have been a
holdover from some previous decade. Nor did it matter very
much that in fact he was peering *clear through the building*
and into the one behind it, and in this way mixing up two
very different sorts of personnel.

He came back, got into his clothes, and gathered up the
blanket. Itself, the book had snapped shut of its own volition
and was edging off stealthily, striving to get out of the light.
Never yet had he been able to accomplish any reading in daylight, not since he had been a clear-headed boy without faults
and capable of hundreds of pages at a time. Suddenly, just then,
half a mile away, an emaciated figure rose up abruptly and began flagging to him deliriously from a rooftop of his own. Lee,
however, ignored it. His attention was upon the burly figure
down below who kept marching back and forth atop the city
wall with a tube or weapon of some kind cradled in both arms.

6

The staircase was unsafe; Lee waited for his eyes to adapt and then, having made a bundle of his book, shoes, and glasses, began to descend into the darkness with its ever-present smell of rotting mice. One bad step and it would mean a five-hundred-foot drop through total blackness and into a pool of liquefied filth. Accordingly, he turned in at the first corridor and tiptoed down past where a bar of light was showing under one of the doors. Here, he knew, there dwelt a certain old man who was so silent at all times, and so self-effacing, that Lee had often wanted to go in and thank him for it face to face. And now, no doubt, the man once more was sitting on the edge of his narrow bed, once more reading in his foreign newspapers, and pausing only for the reason that he could hear Lee listening at the door.

Lee went on. His own apartment had three locks, one of them so idiosyncratic that by the time he got inside he was in a bitter mood. The hall, too, already very tight, had been made nearly impassable by the number of book-cases that ran the length of both walls and continued on

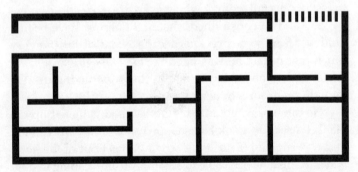

into the complex maze of two dozen rooms, mere cubicles, many of them, that he almost never visited anymore. Here he stood, tapping and humming, while he waited with growing impatience for his eyes to adjust to the obscurity of the place.

In truth, the building had not been designed for residential use in the first place. He tiptoed through the kitchen, and then into the great room where formerly a vast engine of some sort had stood bolted to the floor. These days, he kept this area stocked with books and furniture, a telescope and globe, two desks, and a carpet that was dense enough and good enough to sleep upon. And yet, not even here could he escape the sounds of the street, especially when the door to the balcony had been left ajar. He stepped forward to close it, but then instead went out onto the thing and glanced down into the chasm itself where a tumult had broken out among a crowd of youths who were pushing and yelling—he never could say whether it was serious or not—and carrying their radios around with them. Someday, he knew, this balcony would certainly drop off from its hinges and toss him down into the pullulating mob beneath. Or, that which worried him more, that he would wake someday to find that the city gates had been closed and locked, locked forever, and with an Age of Nightmares coming on. Even now, he could see the watchman in his tin helmet, could see him turn deliberately and then march back slowly in his traces, his sunglasses glinting from half a mile away, his weapon always at the ready.

A haze was up; it had brought with it the salt sea smell that came from Sheep's Head Bay. One hour more and all such smoke and fog would be at liberty to escape off into the encroaching twilight. Nearer at hand, he could see where a building was going up, a gigantic structure formed seemingly out of a "gelatin" that refracted the sun and annealed the moon and mirrored the stars. With all its strangeness, it put him in mind of a certain ziggurat seen in old textbooks. Meanwhile, two miles further, it was already dark enough that lamps could be seen flickering weakly in the cerebellum of the towering apartment complex called "Nietzsche's Head."

He came back, replaced the book, and then, moving silently, peeped in on his wife where—he *always* knew how to find her—she had taken up in the innermost chamber of the maze. Either she would be doing a bit of sewing, or listening to one of her operas, or both, or dithering with her seeds and potted plants. He did so love to come upon her like this, when she was not aware of him, and then to spy in upon her. Thin was her neck, with wisps of hair. Moreover, she had a serious way of bending over her work, so like a child striving to write. He gave twenty seconds to it, but still could not make out what it was she was muttering. Finally, he decided to leave her in peace.

When night was at its deepest, sometimes it fell quiet enough in the city that he could imagine himself back in those centuries he so much liked to read about. He might lie for a full hour, never moving, rejoicing in the thought that soon he would likely be asleep. Indeed, he could remember when he had been able to fall off straightway into a seven- or eight-hour slumber, never to awaken until the yellow sun summoned him out of bed and to a bright new day. But not now, no longer, not since he had passed the age of fifty and had learned to set aside the night for his troubles, and for meditating on them in richer detail than he was disposed to do when the sun was up. Furthermore, he had the unpleasant sensation either that the mattress had been wired to a generator, or else that an insect had gotten into the doorknob and might at any moment start up again with its diurnal noise. All might still have been well, he might yet have rolled off to sleep, had he not been so excited and so self-congratulatory about the prospect of it.

Even then, he did not give up all hope. Forty-five minutes more went by and still he refused to move. The apartment was well constructed—he was confident of that—and most unlikely to collapse out from under him. As for his wife, he wished for her a wonderful sleep full of calm. Moreover, he felt certain that he could find her, no matter what region of the apartment she had withdrawn to. And all in all, he was highly resolved not to awaken her on this night, not unless it came to a worse crisis than he expected.

He gave it another half-hour, his anger rising by leaps when he heard the first faint stirrings of the moth in the door-knob. As if that were not enough, he thought that he could sense the wallpaper straining away from the wall, so ardent was it (and understandably so!) to resume its old position as a coil. Finally (and this was the last touch) he felt that one of his arms was shorter than it ought to be.

He cursed, stood, and then sought about incompetently for the light. His impulse was to go and retrieve a book; instead, to his dismay, he found himself veering off for the television, and even snuggling up to the thing, as if for warmth. At first, he searched the channels for news, but then had finally to settle for a thirty-five-year-old blonde who, though strikingly pretty, was so patronizing and so full of an annoyed impatience, her hair so rain-drenched in accord with the mode, that he hurriedly switched over to a black-headed girl of perhaps thirty-two. The news, however, had ended. Lee now drew closer for the advertisements, including one that featured a certain famous film actor now somewhat past his prime. Lee came closer. Did the man not realize that his career was in tatters? That it were better to retreat from out of the public eye than to be promoting a certain suntan oil? Lee moved on, pausing when he came to a discussion of budgetary and trade problems moderated by a former basket-ball great in tight pants and an earring in one ear. But mostly Lee focused upon the journalists themselves, especially the females of the profession, a new species indeed, as it seemed to him, all of them composed of extreme hauteur, expensive clothing, aggressiveness, and, of course, annoyed impatience.

He turned it off and walked away from it. It was only a few steps to his other room, his alternative sleeping place with its antique bedstead that, however, now that he stood looking at it, seemed to him far too high off the ground. And then, too, he visited here so infrequently, the place had a moribund smell to it. Three books lay on the table, and in them a total of seven bookmarks indicating either where his progress had ended or where certain favorite passages were located.

He passed quietly by the place in which he believed Judy to be resting, and then continued on down to the end of the corridor where he maintained a tiny place, a mere cell really, with scarcely enough area for the pallet (put together out of old quilts), the extra set of eyeglasses, and the half-dozen volumes that served to support the lamp. It did have this one great advantage: that if he should fall out of "bed," it would be a very short drop. Moreover, lying face-down, his heart had nought but solid oaken flooring beneath it, instead of vibrating springs.

He got down in great joy, allowing his mind to clear and his limbs to take pleasure in the firmness of it. Even if he were to hear loud noises, explosions from the lower city, or faint ones, a bat tapping at the glass with black fingers, even then he would not allow it to disturb him, not so long as he could lie face-down, his nose in old quilts that had been fetched all the way from Alabama. He counted, getting to nine before he did in fact pick up a muffled sound that seemed to emanate from New Jersey, miles away. He was doing well. He had a flashlight in case of need, and three books within easy reach. As to the apartment itself, no one could decipher the puzzle of his complicated locks, nor could anyone scale so high above the street and hope to reach the balcony. And yet… And yet… He had to admit it, that it was not *absolutely* infeasible for a daring-enough individual to lower himself from the roof.

He had done well, to come to his third room. He might not actually *sleep*, but he would certainly get some thinking done. Thinking about it, he began whistling. The narrow window permitted him to keen in on one single star only, the largest in the sky. Inevitably, he began to consider the tremendous fields and strangely hued seas that must characterize such an astral body, and how it would have been to pass all one's life amid so many other suns and bright stars.

He had lapsed into dreams, doing well, and yet he must never allow himself to imagine that he was actually asleep as yet, certainly not. No, sleep was a much greater project, requiring time, genius, great suffering, and perfect coordination; thinking about it, he found that he was doing less well than he had believed. And that, of course, was when his heart began squeaking, and then, as he paid closer heed to it, began "thrashing," and then finally, the last stage, began pounding through the quilts and carpet and making reverberations on the floor.

He wanted to cry. One last remedy he had, namely his pistol, which he was not yet however quite ready to use. His favorite star had also vanished, its fields and valleys and murk-enshrouded hills. Soon enough, he knew, the bakers and fishmongers would be hurrying on toward their places of work, to be followed shortly after by the dawn coming up noisily over Long Island Sound. He too, he had just three hours within which to grab off some sleep. Sleep! His own favorite elixir. No one loved it more, and never had anyone been vouchsafed less of it. A single spoonful had the power to get him through an entire day.

He rose, cursing, and then padded on down past where he had thought Judy might be sleeping. His book hoard was vast but incongruous; moreover, the things had been arranged by color and size, and never by contents alone. And if he could sometimes find what he wanted simply by running his finger over it, tonight he had to put on his glasses, take the flashlight, and then kneel down in front of the cabinet and squint through the doors of glass. The books, *they* were doing well, why then could not *he?* True, they were well supported by other members of their own kind, and even the flashlight beam disturbed them not. And such volumes, too! Big things, some of them, with gold dust on the fore-edges; he did not like to think back upon the great efforts (and great risks!) it had cost him to pilfer them one by one from under the nose of the librarian, a naïve man possessed of far more books than he himself would ever need or use. Now, searching with the light, Lee focused upon a certain plum-colored volume that, if he recalled rightly, had come furnished with endpapers that were themselves quite as strange as the book's actual matter. He took it now, opening the thing and getting down on all fours to feed upon the whole curiosity of it.

The book had maps, *colored* maps, and a ninety-year-old advertisement lauding a certain turn-of-the-century cough medicine. Lee saw this too, that the margins were full of some very cogent notes writ in faded pencil, including in one place a heartrending cry of scholarly despair. He drew back, at the same time catching a frightened-looking reflection of himself in the glass door. There, in addition, he had a ten-volume set of the *Report of the Magicians of Ninevah*, tall books full of all the wisdom in the world, provided only that one knew how to read them aright.

He gave half an hour to it, reading slowly and deliberately until finally his mind began to fuzz over. A *real* person would have fallen off to sleep easily by now; instead, his own punishment was only just beginning. He allowed the book to drop and then, shutting both eyes, pretended he too was asleep, as if thus he might trick body and mind into going along. It was wicked, the way his system functioned. In daytime, he could hardly stay awake.

He rose painfully, and then tiptoed down to spy in upon his wife, horrified to find that she was not at all where he had imagined. Quickly he ran around to the far end, cutting in and out of the corridor. She had taken up in the second-largest room in the house, a low-ceilinged affair furnished only with her bed, her machine and opera recordings, and a small clutter of clothing with two elfin shoes (tiny but heavy) parked side by side.

She was sleeping in her fashion, her mouth parted open very slightly in a sort of mild surprise. He felt that he needed only to touch his head to hers in order to fall into her same slumber, which was her specific reward for being the sort of person she was. He came closer, yet not so close as to disturb her. Apart from what went on in that mind and in those memories, he himself had no really verifiable history at all.

And now, he knew that he was going back onto the roof again.

It was the grey building to the west that most oppressed him; it looked to him that it might topple over at any moment, smiting him where he stood. And yet, even at this extreme hour, there were still some four or five clerks laboring dutifully in their cells. He then saw something that he was not supposed to see, namely a very furtive-looking janitress who had parked her mop and locked the door and now was rifling joyously through the file cabinet.

He went around to the northern view and stood gazing down into the slow, silent traffic of dark cars that halted now and again to sniff at the base of the buildings. He saw two vehicles that had come nose-to-nose, and saw further how someone, a woman, he thought, quickly left one car in order to get into the other. Nearer, he saw (and heard) a sudden yellow flareup where, no doubt, one of the over-worked television sets had finally exploded. Indeed, there were all sorts of indications up and down the valley—a furry green lamp sputtering in a second-story apartment, pistol shots, the sound of an animal howling in forlornness and remorse, and then, most gorgeous of all by far, the appearance of a spotlight signaling desperately from a ship at sea. And *this* was the hour his countrymen had set aside for sleeping! Himself, he felt like old Morin looking down onto the doomed city of Uz.

He drank. A scant three hours and he'd be in his suit again, again at his desk and once more nodding and smiling at those whom he loathed. He simply could not understand it, how that after all his youth and confidence, and all the number of books that he had read, that he could have come to this. It was not *his* city, not his epoch either. Suddenly— and here Lee ducked down quickly behind the balustrade—

he caught sight of someone, a little bald-headed gnome who, apparently, had gone out onto the roof next door and was peeping over at him from behind the chimney. Lee cursed. It *never* failed—each time he imagined he was alone, there proved *every time* to be some malevolent little spirit spying on him from one place or another. Again he drank, but kept his eye on the spot where, sooner or later, the gnome would make his mistake.

Possibly, he slept; in any case, he was still in the standing position. The ziggurat, formerly lit up so brightly where the masons had been working on it, now was dark, its scaffolding enshrouded. Beyond the river, he saw one lone glow in "Nietzsche's" brain. Meanwhile, the screaming itself had died away completely, as if the ape or hog, or whatever manner of animal it had been, as if the creature had simply been having bad dreams. Lee moved quietly, taking all care not to excite the silent old foreign man down below, who would be sleeping fitfully among his litter of newspapers. And that was when he spied Judy moving toward him in her green winged robe.

"Can't sleep?"

"Never."

"Oh, God. Want me to rub your back?"

"Drink first, *then* rub."

"Oh, no; no more drink for you, no, no, no. You've already had…"

"One."

"Ha. Why, you've got one right now!"

That was true. Lee looked at it. "What time is it?"

Incredibly, she began to move off, as if to go down below and check on the clock.

"Hold it! I know what time it is."

"How can you tell?"

"The moon. See those dark spots?"

She looked at it, nodding dubiously. Suddenly, he grabbed

her, tickling and sending her off into peals of indignation and laughter. And that, of course, was when the gnome came out of hiding, this time staring at them quite unashamedly through a pair of field glasses.

"Good grief!" said Judy.

"Ignore him."

"Let's go back, Lee."

"Soon, soon." He expected her to go below; instead, she went two steps and then sat, her back to the ledge. He was just as glad she couldn't see it when the lights dimmed throughout the valley before coming back on strong again, proof of a new spate of executions being carried out in a certain downtown building. Now, given the view (so many tattling stars) and the smell (with some little tincture of the ocean in it), his ancient hallucination was coming back, namely that he would very likely leap off some night and go swimming in a stuff stranger than a fluid.

Chapter Two

HE BLUNDERED OUT INTO THE SUN, CURSING. Directly in front of him he saw an eager young man striding off radiantly toward an office building of his own, Lee putting on speed in hopes of stepping on his heel. Such *motivated* people, this new genus of the bonded and insured, the deodorized and manicured—more and more of them were continually coming in from the provinces to help themselves to grand salaries—he would have loved to slay the lot of them.

Suddenly, he found himself marching pace for pace with one of the females of the species, this one rather taller than the average, and exhibiting a thousand dollars' worth of clothes. He followed for two blocks, dodging in and out of the crowd. With her blithe optimism, she appeared not to realize that she was being trailed by one whose upper body strength was at least three times her own. Ah yes, so they had lost all fear of the male, these women had, a very bad sign indeed. Lee groaned, but then decided to let her go her way. Too late, he realized he had strode past his bus stop and must now go back for it. It angered him when he saw the crowd, a band of dawdling thralls, gum-chewers, sports fans, and the like. A lout brushed up against him, Lee enduring it without comment. He *was* somewhat protected by the haze of his own sleeplessness, which put him "at a distance," as it were. Today, at least, the sky was blue, a far better sight than what he saw across the road, namely a living, twitching, nauseating "millipede" composed of ten thousand office workers dressed in shoes.

The bus arrived, stopped, and popped open, giving Lee the chance to worm his way on board well in advance of the mob. Out of old habit, he went straight to the back and placed himself across from a black man glazed over in semi-sleep. Next to him sat a fierce-looking secretary whose skirt was so short that she must keep her legs pasted together in extreme tension, until her poor kneecaps had turned quite white. Lee gazed at the spot deliberately, forcing them tighter still. By his reckoning, it must have been when she was twelve that she first began experimenting with makeup, rouge, eye shadow, and the like. He spent two minutes analyzing her motives (the usual ones) before turning his attention to the Sardinian, or perhaps Greek woman, who sat elbow to elbow with her. This latter, she had been a beauty at one time, no doubt about it, but now had gone to fat. And when he thought of Sardinia itself, or Greece... Better she had stayed in her own good land. Next, Lee examined her legs, puffy things full of veins, and much too short to hit the floor.

The bus gathered speed, breaking into an evil neighborhood where, it seemed to him, the whole population had come pouring out of their apartments in order to stand about and look at one another. One man in particular caught his attention, a seventy-year-old, the saddest he had ever seen, with a punching bag for a belly and a pale blue eye that only now, in this his final year, was beginning to ask questions. But most appalling of all were the youths, dozens upon dozens of them and all of them grinning. Nor could he think about youth in the city without also thinking about grins.

They slowed and then began to pass into the shadow of the ziggurat itself. It had been a long time since any significant progress had gone forward on the thing, with the result that he could see clearly into the fantastical complexity of its comblike interior, a structural tactic made necessary by the unprecedented weight and diameter of the thing. Indeed, it blocked out the sun. One single mason he saw, the world's most intrepid, dangling from the upper stories by a thread.

The following blocks were lined on both sides with flattop office buildings that, to him, looked like Roman war machines with catapults sticking from the roofs. Here, the crowds flowed past in unending sequence, a bacon-and-egg-powered race, responsibly dressed, flooding in from Queens and Long Island and points even further than that, the freest people on earth. But they did not *look* free. Suddenly, he snorted and clapped his hand over his mouth. For hundreds of years, the nations had sent forth their bravest to fight and to die for…

This. He got up and edged to the door, moving in tandem with an enthusiastic thirty-year-old in an expensive-looking tie and a heady lotion. Lee's building might have been exactly like the others but for Sidney's lunch box (an apple in it) set out carefully on the thirty-first-floor window sill. It was the elevator, however, that made him think of turning and going back home again. It had two dozen souls in it, all of them reeking of dry cleaning fluid. Lee *tried* to put on a pleasant face. Suddenly, the door snapped shut, almost catching him by the button. How he abhorred the modern clothing! In this, too, the West had done nothing but go downhill since Byron's time.

Came now the most difficult moment in the day, when he must abandon the elevator and then walk forward down the row of desks without executing a facecrime. Valerie was in place, perhaps had been there two hours already. It was a strange and remarkable truth, that whereas he was twenty years her elder, yet their rank, their salary, and their standing, it was exactly the same.

"And how was *your* weekend?"

Lee tried to look at her. Her voice was lilting, musical, full of irony.

"Lots of wild parties?"

That was it! *That* was the note, he had heard it before, the very voice itself of new-style womanhood in the waning years of a century that had already started out badly enough with Mahler's death. Instead of answering immediately, Lee switched on his computer and allowed it to digest. Finally, smiling sweetly, he said:

"Good morning."

"Oh come now Lee, you know you don't mean it!" She laughed gaily, tossing back her head and emitting a peal of highly sophisticated laughter in the approved manner. Yes, he could believe it, that such a one, with rain-drenched hair, might actually be considered attractive by a new-style man. Indeed he wished them great happiness together, to be promptly followed up by a new-style divorce. Glad was he when the computer cleared, and he no longer had to gaze upon the huge pile of work that the bitch had accomplished already.

The first hour of the week, it fell away quietly enough, leaving but thirty-six more (plus one-half) before he could start over again. Was anyone enjoying this? All over town, the computers were clearing, a vaster army than ever the Assyrians had employed. Suddenly, in great horror, he realized, first, that his face was slipping, and, second, that Valerie had come very close to catching him at it. What he wanted, of course, was to get him up on the desk (it was big enough), and then to fall off to sleep for a few years, awakening new-born and full of relish once the century was over. Instead, he reached into the desk and drew out the next file. His role in life, not to put too fine a point upon it, was to go through these insurance applications one by one, and then to see to it that all those who stood in need of coverage were not vouchsafed any. Sidney, meanwhile, had arrived late and was trying to atone for it by rattling his papers and popping his gum.

The second hour came and then fell away, empowering him to go and fetch a cup of coffee. It was bad policy to be seen retreating into the toilet with a cup in one hand; nevertheless,

20

he ventured it anyway. Happily, the room was empty, a blessing that augured well for the rest of the day. Here, and here alone, he did not have to worry about his face. Unfortunately, he had broken open his hemorrhoids again, the blood and syrup producing a sizzling noise. Someday, he expected to find that he had slipped his whole equipment, heart, lungs, bowels and all, and left it seething in the pot.

No one had been good enough to leave a newspaper for him, wherefore he was reduced to a more in-depth reading of the graffiti. These authors, these rhymers, they simply lacked the talent to be *truly* offensive. Himself, he had brought no crayon with him. Glancing at his watch, he noted that he had two minutes, no more, or else the time-and-motion people would have begun to perceive his absence. At that moment, someone came in and began whistling and urinating in consonance, falling silent when he observed a pair of shoes in one of the compartments. The toilet itself was in a great mess by now, a broth of blood and feces and paper such as would have appalled a torturer; Lee decided to leave it on display.

When midday came, as was its wont between twelve and two, Lee rose up gladly, well intentioned, and then hied him down past the refectory swarming with men in suits, the scum of every business school in North America. And whereas he might be *among* them, and *amid* them (and about to be run over by them too), yet was he not *of* them, not in any true sense. His greatest dread was of being invited in to take a seat and to talk of baseball and gas mileage, of prices, cars, women, taxes, and the rest of it. His practice therefore was to spurt past the opening at high speed—he did so now—and thence to the outside world itself with its sun and clouds.

Every face he saw, it was wooden and unhappy, the authentic twentieth-century misery showing through. Fortunate indeed were they that their employers couldn't see them, not so long as unhappiness be considered a form of insubordination. Himself, he was thinking seriously of fleeing back to his toilet; instead, taking his chances, he leapt into the current, finding a niche for himself. These were strange fish; in front, he had a large man lumping along in an uncomfortable suit, the back of his head imparting the tragic cast of one whose wife loved him no longer. Lee looked all about, even walking backwards for a short space when he saw that he was surrounded by people who in better times might almost have been bookbinders, goldsmiths, ship pilots, bee masters, and others of the humane professions, instead of the "analysts," "consultants" (again, Lee clapped his hand over his mouth), and interest-rate experts that in fact they were. He descried a bosomy woman of the old style, one who might have sufficed excellently as a tavernkeeper's daughter, instead of being the software saleswoman that her briefcase indicated she was. That moment, he stumbled and fell, picking himself up with embarrassment. It was a great error, forever to be watching other people's arms and legs and mistaking them for his own.

It was warm, and yet they crossed in a clump, out of urban habit. Here, a black man, unemployed to judge by him, had strayed down from northernmost Manhattan and, apparently, was viewing William Street for the first time in his career. Lee followed briefly. "Let him get him down South" (said Lee to himself), "where at least he might have a garden and hens." Then: "For it were better by far to abide among an ignorant folk in great heat than to stay here, miserable, encapsulated in a concrete vacuum of asphalt and glass."

There was at that time a certain restaurant where the food was deleterious and the service poor, and where he was sure of finding an empty booth. Furthermore, he admired the waitress, one of the very few truly lazy persons still in evidence anywhere. Now, instead of coming forward as he entered, she simply smiled, and then went on thumbing through her magazine. Slowly and slowly, year after year, he had built up his credit with her, so much so that when he happened to fall off to sleep in his own favorite booth, yet he could always rely upon her to awaken him in time. Today, he had brought a book with him, a most curious one detailing certain recent excavations in and around the giant city of Mycenaean Gla. His stomach, however, was behaving badly, and continued to burble even as he read.

Now finally the woman did come, bringing his preferred brand of soup.

"I brought your chowder."

"Yes!" (Lee could see that she had brought it. Unfortunately, she was a gum-chewer. He smiled sweetly while she sank down on the bench across from him.)

"How is it out there?"

"Outside? Unbelievable." (She too was from the South; she too could not adhere to city ways.)

"Pshaw, I see 'em coming by here all day long. Big hurry! What's the matter with these people, Lee?"

"I don't know."

"Some of these fellows never even been fishing in their whole life."

"Nothing surprises me, not anymore."

"Got yourself a book there!"

"Yes, I do; yes. But I can't read and talk at the same time."

"And some of 'em! How come they look so…?"

"How come they look the way they do?"

"Yeah! Why, Lee? Is it because…?"

He nodded sadly.

"You know, I kind of feel sorry for them."

"Not me."

"Me neither! Now just for instance, look at that one."

Lee looked. (The book he had returned to his pocket.) Outside, a duck-like individual was waddling past at great speed, his eye upon some spiritual fulfillment that, apparently, was looming brightly at the end of Broad Street. Impossible not to laugh, even Lee too, who really preferred to sleep.

"Yes, this is the heyday of such types, Louise. Now when *I* was in school, we used to beat up people like that. So! And now, I think I'd like to take a nap, a short one."

She left him. Lee hastened to finish up with the chowder, which, in truth, apart from a rather adorable little seahorse that had somehow gotten caught in the net, contained but one single oyster of any real size. Lee looked at it, turning it with the spoon. Surely these were the strangest of all animals, and had the least integrity; based upon his knowledge, he ascribed them to the late Devonian, his own special favorite among the greater epochs.

He now consumed the one oyster, chomping down quickly lest it have still some life in it. Louise had been kind enough to draw the shade for him, and he felt that he could look forward to a good fifteen-, or perhaps twenty-minute nap; instead, of course, that was when two businessmen opted to come inside and set up at the table nearest to him. Lee groaned, doing it loudly. Their presence animated the girl who up until now had been sitting quietly in the rear. The men in suits, they liked her legs, while as for the girl, she liked their prospects, the nearest thing to love still available. Finally Lee pried open the book and read two paragraphs more before he admitted that he was not absorbing anything. Outside he could hear shouting, followed by a deep rollicking laughter. No one, he knew, made a noise like that in New York City unless someone was getting hurt. That was when the girl (of Brooklyn, he judged) shifted in her chair, a slow procedure that showed her underwear. She believed—and the world told her so—that all good things revolved around the mucous on her pad.

He walked back in a trance, carried along in the flood of the condemned. At William Street, the curbs were lined with immense black limousines with chauffeurs, each one more cynical looking than the other. It was seldom that, as now, he managed to view one of the actual passengers, in this instance a rather mild-looking man whose mouth, however, resembled a rectum. Lee came closer, till man and driver shooed him away.

Lee strode right past the bookstore and went on for another twenty yards before resigning himself, turning, and coming back. The window had two primary sorts of literature in it, one type telling how to get rich and the other telling how to get thin. The shop *he* craved would have been dim, with perhaps a cat sleeping in front of the fire, and all of it presided over by a polyhistor in dense glasses; instead, this place, germless as a ward, was lit up so brilliantly that it hurt the eyes. As for the saleswoman... She had more lief undergo major surgery than open a serious book.

He had given up on fiction and yet, despite everything, he found himself once more padding over to the shelves and taking down the first volume that, as he should have known in advance, contained the marriage-and-divorce confessions of yet another thirty-five-year-old with a degree from Smith. He checked for her photograph... Ah yes! she *did* have that snottiness and hauteur—he couldn't deny it—and it was no wonder the publishers were so excited. Suddenly Lee jumped back, disconcerted to find that two (not one) snotty-looking thirty-five-olds had joined him at the counter and were pouring through the stuff with avidity.

He moved downrange. Here, far out of sight, he had tucked away for safekeeping a rather poorly printed edition of Burton's *Melancholy*, very possibly the last surviving copy this side of the Atlantic. Now, hand trembling, he opened and then read the better part of a full page of it. That was when the girl came running up.

"Is there something you *want?*"

"Umm? No, the reason I'm down on the floor is because..."

"Oh God. Well, do you intend to *buy* it?"

Lee checked the price. "Give you a dollar for it."

"Ohhh!"

She was gone. It gave Lee the opportunity to stick the book into his pants, where, in truth, it was profoundly uncomfortable. Furthermore, the girl had left a ballpoint pen behind, which he took as well.

He came in wearing a face that was pleasant, until he saw how much Valerie had accomplished in his absence. These new people! They seemed to grow only the more energetic as the day drew on. Never ceasing to work, she asked:

"Have yourself a lovely lunch?"

He nodded.

"You didn't go to that place!"

Lee blushed.

"Splurging again! And were the chitterlings good today?"

His chin trembled. He had no weapon at hand, nothing. Sidney, meanwhile, was whistling through his teeth. He had a high school ring and a pot belly, and now soon they'd be turning him loose as one unable to keep up with Val's new pace.

Sometimes he was able to sleep on the bus, that is to say until the realization of what he was doing brought him out of it each time. Already they had navigated the Latin slum and now were deep into the black; he gave thanks for today's driver, a man so artful that he could bring the bus safely through a crowd of rock-throwing children. Suddenly, an enormous woman ran out into the street, hailing and shouting for the driver to stop. Instead, the bus went around her and began to move much faster.

There were approximately a hundred yards between the street and his building, but before he could stroll the whole distance, night came crashing down upon the town, bringing with it the moon, neon, airplanes, and five bright stars bouncing on the western roofs. He ran for the elevator, finding it vacant—or so he imagined, until he got on board and discovered an alarmed old woman huddling in the corner. The mechanism itself was faulty, with the result that they must halt at every separate story and waste some ten seconds in gazing in upon the poor—fat men in undershirts, women with babies—who stood gazing back at *them*. Very glad was he when at last he leapt out onto his own floor, leaving the woman to ride down again and to review in solitude the same seventeen scenes that they had just reviewed together.

Never yet had anyone dared to trespass down into his own part of the corridor; nevertheless, Lee now got down on one knee and began to adjust the tripwire (plain common thread) that he had rigged with so much patience. Itself, the door was locked—good. He loved to come in silently and squeeze between the bookcases. For it was only in this way that he could hope to catch his wife speaking to herself in her dark fashion.

"Yi!" She leapt. He waited for her to grow calm again before he boasted: "Well, we did it: only four more days and it'll be the weekend again."

"Was it bad?"

He shrugged. Already she had opened the bottle of vodka, a clear stuff that promised oblivion. It looked good to him, this time of day.

Night did come, and intoxication too, but still he could not sleep. Finally, toward two, he rose and blundered about for a time before heading down to Judy's room. At first, she looked like old Placidia half-seated in her sturdy crypt, until he drew up near enough to see that in fact it was his own pretty wife. Her fingers, so tiny they served a cosmetic function only, were looped over the covers. Lee came nearer, pondering on her form and nature, and especially her delicate skull that seemed to offer only just enough shelter to protect its contents against the weather. And if she was awake and whispering to him (and she was), yet he could understand none of it.

Taking his bottle with him, he stepped out onto the balcony, where he was immediately swept up by the beauty of it. He could not say which was most gorgeous—faint blue sky with stars, or dark field with its thousands of campfires.

Someday this too would be nothing but descriptions in old unread books. He could envision the scholars of the future, insouciant men speaking patronizingly and with many a snort about this wasting epoch, the only one he had.

He lit a cigarette and tossed the match off into the current. Northwards, two searchlights with pencil-thin beams were raking frantically across the sky, while nearer—Lee was shocked—someone had mounted all the way to the peak of the ziggurat and was signaling with a lantern. A boat was traveling very slowly upriver; Lee saw how the steersman, a tall man, was able to hand off a toll, or message, to the woman waiting on shore. Meanwhile, in the next building, an undressed man on the fortieth floor was slumped in a chair while staring at a screen that had gone inert. A fight had broken out below, some five or six of them shoving and shouting and laughing. *He* wanted sleep, *they* wanted... What? All might still have been well had not then a sudden burst of "music" broken out in the canyon where, it seemed to him, he could actually see people dancing wildly around one of the fires. He cursed, groaned, called, and then, coming forward, pulled out his thing at last and commenced to piss down gleefully into the ululating Jebusites beneath.

Chapter Three

HE TUMBLED OUT INTO THE LIGHT, BUT THEN PICKED HIMSELF UP HASTILY AND HEADED OFF TOWARD THE NORTH. After but two hours of sleep, this was to be his last day on earth.

It was his policy to be unpredictable, in order that no one should come to learn his route. Today, therefore, after waiting seven minutes for the bus, he turned suddenly and went down into a hole in the ground. Today, the people were surly, but not yet dangerously so. He passed a deranged person singing hymns, and then next—and this did surprise him—saw two well-dressed businessmen climb down from the platform and then go trundling off slowly and sadly into the tunnel itself. Suddenly, a train came running into the station and then, never slowing, ran back out again, leaving Lee with the memory of five thousand suits dangling from the hooks.

He could feel a headache coming on. Among this ruck, these tides of men, perhaps the Godhead had implanted a few souls here and there. He saw a boy carrying two books, an encouraging vision, until he realized that the youth was simply taking a course in business administration. Another train had come in meanwhile and had parked, emitting a whole population of determined-looking people quite prepared to grind to dust anyone foolish enough to stand against them. A crowd like that, they need only be armed with pea-shooters in order to constitute an invincible army. Himself, he took refuge in a tiny little shop (not much bigger than a closet) that catered to philatelists.

It was wonderful stuff, thousands upon thousands of brightly colored stamps from all parts of the world. He found himself face to face with a certain well-known African dictator whose face had been reproduced on a series of particularly lovely stamps with images of giraffes romping on a background bordered with silver gilt. Next, coming nearer and taking off his glasses, he saw where some of the very best panels of some of Bosch's very finest paintings had been reissued by one of the world's smallest countries. And now, changing yet again into his *other* glasses, far the more powerful of his two sets, he believed that he could make out details of the medieval experience, including a far-away scene of an old-style wind-mill and what looked like the minuscule figure of a villain hanging from one of the paddles. He could have seen so much more but for the proprietor—a fat man, *too* fat for the tiny shop, whose mouth was cruel and whose eyes had an extinct look.

"Bosch!" said Lee, pointing to it. "Nothing surprises me anymore."

"You like that, do you?"

Lee nodded. His attention, however, had shifted to Bohemia and Moravia, and to an extraordinary series that pictured the city of Prague when Prague was in its best days. These things had a delicacy to them, not to mention a peculiar faded quality, like antique wallpaper. Fortunately, the precious little things had been mounted on a card that would slip in and out of his pocket with a grace. But even under such favorable circumstances, he still had to wait until another customer, a mere wide-eyed boy dazzled by the array, came in and claimed the man's attention.

Instead of coffee, Lee had used his time for pilfering stamps, an excellent method for further confusing anyone hoping to memorize his habits. Now he drifted back to the platform, dawdled about in seeming indifference, and then at the last split instant leapt aboard the train. Unhappily, he had thus put himself face to face with a chubby little businessman whose face, with its two baby cheeks and bright red mouth, looked like a pair of buttocks sitting athwart a neck. Nothing could have overmastered the sweet smell that emanated from the man, the result of a high-priced lotion, Lee had to assume, that had aged a great while alongside the man's best wines. After a minute of it, with the two of them pretending to look past each other, Lee let his own face fall quite away to reveal the true one that lay at all times just beneath the surface. At once, the man spun and faced the other way. It required some strength (so thick was the crowd) for Lee to free his left arm and then, working with patience and gentleness, to hoist the man's wallet, a painstaking job that he carried off with aplomb and without even thinking about it overmuch. But of all the amazements of this particular morning, nothing amazed Lee more than this, namely that *the man knew he was being robbed, and yet feared to do anything about it*!

The train halted, giving the businessman his chance to waddle off into the crowd where, perhaps, he might have some chance of replacing his wallet, assuming he could find someone even more pusillanimous than he. Himself, Lee put the thing in his vest and then, taking his book, had begun to read when he observed that the woman next to him had fallen asleep on her feet, and that her mouth had lapsed open to reveal a very bad collection of teeth indeed. She would *not* like to see herself in this presentation, not if she still hoped to snare a husband. Lee thought about it, opting not to awaken her just yet. And then, too, he was somewhat worried about the man at his side, a hard-looking quantity with jowls and wattle, and so adept at money-making that his very nose had developed a horrid little stalk with a claw on it.

Lee got out and began hewing through the crowd. Somehow a child had gotten mixed up in the crunch and was being swept downstream; Lee caught a last look at the mute terror on a tiny face that came up no higher than the businessmen's belts. As for the women, Lee questioned how they could endure it, considering the soft character of their bodies and the jewelry that could so easily be snatched away. Further down, an emergency had apparently broken out on the platform itself; he could hear at least three voices, including an impressive baritone giving out a paean to woe. The sound of it followed Lee all the way to the surface and even then continued to issue out through the grates.

He was glad to get to his own building. Or would have been glad, had not the elevator been as jammed as it was. Lee groaned, but then did choose at the last moment to leap on board anyway and face the wall. (In the land where *he* came from, people usually reserved some choice as to who might be pressing up against them.) After a certain distance, he began to fidget—a bad sign. It meant that soon he would begin to hum, a habit that began each time he whizzed past the twenty-eighth floor.

He came out, smiling wildly, and then paced down hurriedly to the men's room and his own personal booth. The wallet possessed a marvelous heaviness that explained itself once he saw how much money it held—a good hundred dollars and more, most of it comprised of General Sherman's ruthless portraitures. Somehow he knew in advance that the man would carry a picture of his wife with him, in this case a mediocre-looking woman with haunted eyes. Better he had photographed her clothed. As for the rest, it was all standard stuff, cards and memberships and the like, most of which he flushed down the hole. The stamps he did *not* flush; they put him in mind of better days, when the whole world had had the rare faint and faded quality of classic postage. Now, bringing the loveliest of them up to his eye, he felt he could almost fall back into the sixteenth century itself, and wander for days. Slowly, his heart began to settle and his mind grow calm again. He was able to leave off humming. And now that he was richer by a hundred dollars, he could feel a sleepiness coming on.

Days passed, or years; he only knew that when finally he came awake, he was on the toilet still. Quickly he hurried out into the office proper, but only to discover the area depopulated and even Valerie herself absent and missing. They were rare and marvelous moments, these precious times when he was able to slumber away the entire morning and yet come awake in time for lunch. Humming, he again checked both wallets, moving some of the bills from one to the other and then forcing both into the same back pocket. Seldom, seldom indeed had he felt himself so rich, and seldom, very seldom, had he ever enjoyed so revivifying a snooze, so free of dreams.

Going to the elevator, he dropped down to the road and sauntered two full blocks before he recognized that he was aiming in the wrong direction. Some of the account executives (he could see them) had joined hands and were piping away merrily down Broad Street. Having retraced his path, he ducked into the pharmacy and stood for a moment gazing down into the magazines on display. He had long been wroth about this, the emaciation of these modern "beauties" that adorned magazine covers. *He* liked meat-and-potatoes women, middle-aged, with bosoms and hips.

It was not his day, not his country, not his epoch; moreover, he had a twelve-year-old boy standing next to him in a business suit. Together, they looked down into the magazines. Lee was at all times conscious of the chemist, a nervous sort of man who wore opaque glasses and had sulfur on his nose. They looked at each other briefly, till the man weakened and glanced away.

One could read much in a nation's medicines; here, the main thing was gas and the science of constraining it. Lee moved on, coming next to a tiny rotating kiosk hung with a brilliant array of suppository cartridges. These were còstly enough, to be sure, but also suited out in a cellophane packaging that slipped almost joyfully into his pocket. He could have taken a dozen of them; instead, he contented himself with less than half that number. There were analgesics too, and each variety of headache had its own special capsule. He took two bottles, one of which held an ovaline pill that was faintly pink and bore a label on it with a picture of the moon. Suddenly, he turned and glared at the chemist, whose vision was not as poor as he had believed. Now, head held high, Lee marched out past the cashier.

For three blocks he slogged on, speaking to himself bitterly. He had no faith in the city, least of all in the sidewalk that, it seemed to him, was probably not much thicker than a sheet of paper. He tried to guess where the underlying struts might offer some support, and even then he insisted on going upon tiptoes. The Christian Science Reading Room came up, Lee pressing at the window and then exclaiming out loud when he descried a chair that seemed to be vacant. Now, entering with dignity (his face serene), he raced for it, arriving just in time to thwart an older man who simply didn't have the speed, and who looked at him with a hurt expression.

At once, Lee began to nod off to sleep. The chair itself was good and plump, and sometimes (but not today) he had been able to fish out small coins that had slipped between the cushion and the frame. On one side, he had a grand-motherly woman knitting happily in the sun, and on the other, a black man silently tending to a wound on his head where, apparently, someone had popped it open for him. And that was when Lee saw something else, something that caused him to seize up and to hide behind his newspaper—the unspeakable Valerie and two others of the same kind who, between them, were taking up the whole sidewalk. Strange, these were the most modern people on earth, and yet they were all now shrieking and laughing and throwing up their hands precisely in the high fashion of fifty years ago. One girl, the tallest, had the most insouciant laugh of all. He knew this much, that if their clothes were conspicuously conservative, yet they were by no means self-effacing. Indeed the very tilt of their heads proved how very… That was when they began to move away.

Lee leapt from his place. Unfortunately, the old man once more proved too slow, and again a new arrival ended up with the chair. Outside, Lee drew his ballpoint pen (as if he thought to slay all three with it) and then set off after the women with a craftiness that rendered him all but invisible. After two blocks, he was able to hide behind a large woman loaded down with bundles. They crossed in tandem, Lee having to slow and come back for them, and then to circle in seeming indifference while the one he called "Entropy" turned to say a word to "Surfeit," who threw up both of her hands. His soul trembled. Thoughts came to mind, memories of his own dear grandmother who had toiled herself to death with mules. And now these thin ones were wearing the clothes and laughing the laugh that had been paid for by his Alabama grandmother, who had never laughed at all. But by far the most sophisticated of them was Valerie herself, whom Lee named "Anomie" for her character, and her location in history.

He put on speed, crossing over at last into the nasty little park that sat at the tip of Manhattan where the ferry was wont to park. Here, among the denatured pigeons, the three of them came finally to bench. Lee circled behind them, twice darting in close enough to use the pen, but losing heart each time. Again they laughed, laughed most gaily, as if the collapse and ruin of a four-thousand-year-old civilization were the most hilarious thing in the world. Lee moved off some forty yards and seated himself next to a bald-headed man who had fallen off to sleep with a pigeon in his lap. All these people, office thralls from the high buildings, all of them were utterly depleted looking, all of them congealed and glassy and each sitting off by him- or herself staring into his or her own favorite direction. Himself, Lee found that he was gazing over the waves and into the very face of the monstrous "Statue of Liberty," a Pharaonic spirit in the female aspect, as cold and remorseless as outer space. He could feel a headache coming on. "Anomie" was laughing.

He changed positions, putting himself where he could not be seen by the monument but *could* keep watch upon Valerie and her friends. Here, he might almost have fallen off to sleep himself, but for the eerie ambience of the place, which warned him against any such incaution. Not that he was afraid of being robbed! Not while he carried another man's wallet! Rather, it was the sight of so many hundreds of dispirited people in suits, their intellects ruined by office work; it saddened him to see how they filed one by one onto the ferry, each in turn handing over a toll to the smiling pilot, a man so thin he looked to be composed of bones alone.

And yet, he *did* sleep, if only for a moment. Such moments were to be treasured. Suddenly, a great horror sweeping over him, he rose and checked for Valerie. Far away, he heard a bell tolling, a golden sound that, however, summoned neither farmer nor cattle, nor yet the sheep from the hill. Right well enough he knew whom it summoned, as did also the stultified figures scattered among the benches; at once, half a hundred of them stood and began to shake the crumbs out of their laps. Lee, too, he replaced the ballpoint pen. And that was when he set eyes for the first time upon the criminal sitting just across from him, a bad person in rich clothes who, apparently, was trying to simulate the office workers.

Lee sank back down, ruminating on the face of the bad man who refused to look his way. (*Lee's* gaze had four thousand books behind it.) Weakness he saw, and cruelty too; he looked for, but could not absolutely verify, a pistol in a holster that would itself be worn within the vest. And then, too, there was something in the very shape of the man's head, as if the midwife, having seen what was aborning, as if she had tried to forestall it with her foot. Lee began laughing.

"Aw, man!"

"No, no, sorry. No, I was just…"

"Aw, man. What do you *want* from me, huh? Do I know you?"

"No, no. Well not *literally*, of course. However... No, I *am* sorry." (He could not stop laughing. No doubt, it was the wounded innocence in the boy's face, he who had *never* been innocent. Also there was something in his tie and in his socks that showed that he had not, and probably could not, absorb the authentic bourgeois aesthetic.) "Sorry." Then: "May I?"

"Free country."

Lee went and sat next to him. "We can speak with so much more candor like this. As opposed to yelling at each other across the open space."

"Aw, man. Why do I got to talk to you, huh? What, you a cop or something?"

"Ha! No, no. No, no, no. No, I just..."

"And another thing: where the hell are you *from*, man? *England*, for Christ's sake?"

"England! No, no, I..."

"Hold it! Don't be getting too close, OK? I don't like that."

"Sorry. No, I'm from Alabama actually."

"Aw, man! Ala-what? I *knew* there was something, soon as I saw you. OK, tell me this, man, what the hell you doing way down here anyway? Huh?"

Lee started to answer.

"And what's this *laughing* all the time? I don't know man—I gotta say this—you make me kinda nervous."

"Want the rest of this sandwich? It was just lying here."

"Hell no. Hell no I don't want any goddamn sandwich, hell no. Jesus! Now I *am* nervous."

"We don't wear ties like that, not with girls on them."

"Don't like girls, is that what it is? Get out of here, man. Christ!"

"No, no, you misunderstand me. No, actually I just wanted to make a proposal, namely that..."

"'Proposal?' You're sick, man. No, you need to see somebody about that."

"*Business* proposal."

"What?"

"Business."

"I'm listening." He looked off into the extreme distance, his ear keen and his face showing a spiritual expression. Instead of speaking, Lee now took the wallet, drew out the larger bills, and then gave the boy a long lingering look at them.

"OK, man, you made your point. Now put that shit away before somebody…"

"Steals it?"

They both laughed. Lee felt they were getting along very well now. Coming nearer, he whispered:

"There's *nothing* you wouldn't do, is there?"

"I wouldn't say that."

"You'd probably even be willing to…"

"Naw."

"Alright. But a good *beating*, that much you *would* do. Am I right?"

The boy looked off. He carried a little white scar that peeped in and out of his too-tight collar.

"Don't be looking at that scar all the time, OK?"

"Sorry." (Again he could hear the bell tolling distantly, this time a sound more of iron than of gold. He had five minutes, no more, to complete his dealings with the thug at his side.) "How much to give somebody a good beating?"

"How much you got?"

"I got some."

"How much."

"Hundred dollars."

"Jesus shit! That'll get you a busted jaw, *maybe*. If you're lucky."

Lee thought about it. The boy, however, had been able to read his mind.

"No 'credit,' not a chance. Don't even think about it."

"Busted jaw?"

"Right."

"How would you do it?"

"I'll do it. Show me the hundred."

"Busted?"

"Yeah, yeah. Come on, I ain't got all day."

Lee paid, digging out the bills and then, finally, counting out the coins while the criminal remained looking down into the stuff with disbelief.

"Eight quarters. I'm the baddest man there is, and now I got me eight quarters and a goddamn pile of ones. Maybe I ought to break *your* jaw, asshole. Alright, alright, who's the lucky guy?"

"Not a 'guy.'"

"Yeah? Hey, this is getting interesting. Maybe I won't even charge nothing for this. Who's the lucky cunt?"

"Why, she's right where she's supposed to be. See?"

He returned in a splendid frame of mind, even at one point breaking out into a series of little hops and jumps that amazed the underwriters. Already Valerie was in place—how she had arrived before him he could not imagine—and already she had accomplished a very great deal, to judge by how her computer was glowing. These new people! Lee was courteous to her however.

Night did come at last, his own favorite season. For half an hour he lay on his own favorite couch. Now he would either get some reading done, or else fall asleep. In the former case, he might learn something, while if the latter came true... It was too good a prospect to dwell upon. In any case, the volume itself was a great pleasure, an ambrosial heap (hinges weak) with corruption about the edges. The typeface too, he approved it. It had that archaic horror of the German *fractur*, and carried him back in mind to the age of von Kleist and the others. In truth, he did not know whether it was wisdom, or the thought of it, or indeed wisdom's vehicle (books) that most excited him. Or simply the whiff of ink on paper. This one had a map in it; he unfurled it now and lay looking up into the baffling locations—an extinct lake in the middle of nowhere, a thin blue trail that stumbled off into the hot desert before petering out altogether. Nor could he conjure the number of persons who had carried out faultless lives in just such places, the sincere ones whom History had passed over without text. And now it was too late, too late for these and too late for those, and too late for Morin of Bright Eyes who kept the goats of Gla, etc., etc., and now Lee slept.

When he rose, most of the television sets that normally kept the town bathed in colors, most of them were shut off, and the viewers themselves, he assumed, had long ago drawn off into their special cells, there to pass full seven hours in puerile sleep—it made him mad. And yet…and yet… It *was* after all *their* town and never his own. If he had his way the world would have been an aesthetocracy in which ordinary people were treated as utensils. He wanted a small world getting smaller, of a fine people getting finer. And then, too, he had resolved many years ago either to pursue power absolute without limit, either that or else have nothing whatsoever to do with people.

He went back and put on the last movement of Mahler's last symphony, a therapeutic exercise that sometimes (and sometimes not!) reconciled him to his sleeplessness. And in truth, he needed all the genius of Europe to prepare him for another American day.

He played it twice, beauty on top of beauty, and then turned on his side, hoping to float for the next several hours in a sort of "cream." Astonishingly, he actually did feel for a brief time that he might be able to… Oh no. No, no, no; the evil half of him would never permit it—the very idea! A good night's sleep? Ten thousand devils left off what they were doing and rushed forward to prevent it.

He cursed, groaned, wept, but then finally did rise up off the floor and begin calling for his wife. It embarrassed him that his own television—he had been studying the commercials—that it also was still burning in the night. Lee came nearer, as if hoping to be able to read a heavenly message in the recondite code of colloids battering at the screen. But it was bad upon the eyes.

As to where Judy might be sleeping… He calculated that she had most probably retreated down into the further end, there where she kept her wretched little collection of shells and pine cones, and other such relics saved over from an earlier time in their history together. He moved cautiously, until it became necessary to strike the cigarette lighter. Even in sleep she was worrying, worrying about *him*, she who used to fall off into moist slumber devoid of dreaming. Her arm was hanging free, and she seemed to be clutching something in one of her divine hands. It was on account of these hands indeed, perfect as they were, that she might have been acclaimed the world over; instead, she had squandered them in fixing his meals and in soothing him off to sleep. Only now did he realize that she had been looking back at him with open eyes for the past minute.

"Shall we go up onto the roof?"

Lee considered it.

"Want me to read to you?"

"Read what?"

"Whatever you want."

"Naw."

"Have you had a drink?"

"Six."

"O! What's going to happen to you Lee?"

"I don't know. I've been thinking I might go back into mutual funds."

"Oh sure! And what about those certificates?"

"Naw, they don't know who took 'em."

"We could go away."

He wasn't sure that he had heard her correctly. "Now did I hear…?"

"Down south. I know you've been wanting to."

"South! It would never work of course."

"That land you inherited…"

"'Land.' There's nothing on that land."

"There's a house on it. I know because you told me so!"

"'House.' It's a hundred years old!"

"We could fix it."

"Oh? You're good at that sort of thing then?"

"*You* could do it."

Lee snorted. The woman was sitting up and looking at him. These days, she went to bed in full clothing, so as to be prepared at all times for the roof.

"In the South, one can stay up all night, reading and listening to music."

"All night." (He said this dreamily. Somewhere a fire had broken out in the further city where Nietzsche's profile seemed to be staring at it with fascination. Of course, he had to admit that it was not *entirely* like Nietzsche. Nor had it ever been so denominated by anyone save himself.)

"…and do it before we're too *old*," his wife was saying.

"I don't feel old, not when we're talking about leaving New York."

"And do it before they come looking for us!"

"Before the whole rotten system collapses in upon itself?"

"No, before it doesn't."

She was right, Lee had to admit it. And yet still, he couldn't quite believe that anything good could happen, not now, not with both of them into their fifty-second year. His attention was captured by two television sets that had just sprung to life in the opposite apartment, one of which was showing frontal nudity while the other, apparently a mere security system, seemed to be broadcasting an empty hallway. "Music" had erupted in the street below. Not until Lee put on his robe and then went out onto the balcony was he able to make out the cause of it—a radio fixed to the head of a person who was dead or overdosed and lying face-down fifty floors below while exposed to the traffic and the chill, and to the buzzards already on the wing.

Chapter Four

HE CAME POURING OUT OF THE BUILDING, RAN PAST THE DOORMAN (WHO HATED THE SIGHT OF HIM), AND THEN DASHED FORWARD ANOTHER FOUR BLOCKS BEFORE HE REALIZED THAT HE HAD COME AWAY WITHOUT BENEFIT OF TIE. Three nights with no sleep! To him, the people all looked as if they had diseases. Next, he leapt aboard the bus, but then, recollecting which day it was, came off again and headed for the subway. In front, two women of the new type were striding on, completely oblivious that they were passing through the very intersection where someday his new-world guillotine array would be typing out its lovely tune. Suddenly he gave a little hop and began to whistle. He was dreaming, of course, dreaming once more that he was trodding down a road cobbled with human faces.

He toiled one hour exactly and then rose and smiled and was ambling down toward the toilet when he saw that today's sensitivity session for the typists had already been convened in Room 101. He squirted past the opening, hiding momentarily behind a column. His own group was also wont to meet on Wednesdays; however, he had already missed so many convocations that he had come to think of himself as having been recused, so to speak. And then, too, his own sensitivity was already pretty generally recognized among the underwriters.

He came out whistling, but only to jump back once more behind his column when he saw yet another meeting in preparation just across the hall. The room had two analysts in it (one of each gender) together with the company's lead facilitator supported by her amanuensis, a frightened-looking quantity in tinted glasses. Lee, wearing a pleasant face, tried to step quickly past the opening, an effort that failed.

"Pefley!" For a moment Lee stood hesitantly in the doorway, disconcerted to see a dagger on the table pointing toward him, until he realized it was nothing but the letter opener.

"I could come back later."

"Pefley! Well at least we won't have to drag you out of the toilet this time. Come on, come on, this session is for you alone. We've got lots of ground to make up, lots. And close the door, too. Where's your tie?"

Lee blushed. The leader of the team was a largish man, phlegmatic to a degree. He had, however, authored two separate books on his special subject, one for each gender.

"Well…"

"Never mind about the tie, let's get started. Linda? Do you want to lead off?"

Lee looked to her, a thin girl in steel glasses, angry as thunder but yet colder than snow. She had a very orderly stack of papers in front of her, with what looked like a phrenological chart sitting on top. She was speaking, but Lee could hardly hear it. Finally, he held up his hand.

"Ahh… I can barely hear what you're saying."

"Yes? Well that's the way it is with you isn't it? Other people? Taking into account *their* needs and not just your own?"

Lee thought about it, frowning deeply. He could never frown as deeply as the boy on his right, the team's junior member. Looking at him sideways, Lee reckoned his age to be somewhat less than one-half his own. The boy, however, possessed a pipe, and was so eaten up by such extreme

seriousness that it threatened to make an old man of him
in advance of his time. Fascinated, Lee went on staring at him.

"…peer group," said the girl.

Lee nodded. "Right. I've been considering our last meeting, and I think maybe… Know what I mean? Better rapport?"
(He nodded vigorously.) "Role models! Interpersonal relations."

"He's doing it again."

The leader sighed, took off his glasses, and then began
working the thin of his nose. Finally, stretching forth his hand:

"May I have your Mission Statement please? Pefley? You
have it, don't you?"

"Mission? He still hasn't even done his Targets and
Goals yet!"

"Oh boy."

"I did do my Aims however."

"Oh boy. We've been through it and through it, a hundred
times! The *Goals*, Lee, they have to stand *behind* the Aims
and *profile* it, so to speak. Otherwise, it just doesn't work."

"Goals."

"Right."

He wrote it down. The boy to his right had a furrowed
look. Both men feared the girl. "The reason I'm not wearing
a tie is because…"

"Oh come off it, Pefley! We've heard it before, a thousand times. It's not what you *say* that impresses us—you'll
say anything—but rather…"

"What he's *thinking*."

"Precisely. We need to ferret that stuff out and put it on
the table. Right, Pefley?"

"It'll make you feel so much better."

"Precisely! Thanks, Linda. 'Feel better.' All those little
prejudices. Come on, Lee! Let's put 'em on the table, shall we?"

Lee nodded. "That's the only way to do it. How else
can we *treat* this stuff, if we can't *see* it?"

"He's doing it again."

Lee looked at her. The area about her eyes had taken on a bleached look; moreover, her hand was trembling just enough for him to detect it.

"We can't do it for you," said the boy. "You have to do it for yourself. Oh, I know it can be tough! Look at me, I used to have negative feelings about lots of things."

"Naw," said Lee. "I can't accept that."

"But I worked at it, Lee. And now I'm like you see me to be."

"And a much happier person for it, too. Right, Steve?"

"I'd like to be happier," said Lee. "More productive. International competition—we really don't have much choice, do we? No, certainly not; we're all going to have to work together, or else… And Valerie thinks so too."

"Oh God."

Lee grinned. There was a long and mournful silence while the leader of the group stared with anguish into his face. The others, the boy and girl, they were each looking at the two several sides of his head.

"Oh, I don't know. You work for this rather wonderful organization and yet… They don't like to let people go; they consider it a *defeat*."

Lee nodded. "It's not as if I don't have role models. Lots!" (Strangely, he found that he too was frowning in the same deep and profound way as the twenty-three-year-old at his side. They looked at each other. The boy's gaze might have had only four books behind it and yet, because the books were on *management*… Lee flinched and looked away. The girl meanwhile had turned thinner, colder, paler, and better dressed, seemingly, than even of five minutes ago. She had taken out two pens and one pencil, and was arranging and rearranging them on the table, as if sorting through the rot that lay in Lee's soul.)

He hurried back to check on Valerie and then, finding her working cheerfully with her jaw intact, he dashed to the elevator and ascended to a higher floor. Many years had gone by since last he had visited at this particular level; now, in order to show off their knowingness, the management had tacked up a few modernistic paintings along the wall.

Sidling to the office door, he knocked once, delicately, but then suddenly leapt inside, hoping to catch the secretaries in a state of unpreparedness. He had seen it before, how those who assist the great tend to take on great qualities themselves.

"Could I see Mr. Finch?"

"Do you have an appointment?"

"In fact…"

"He doesn't."

They looked as if they had both been hit by the same awful odor. Lee grinned. The young one was pretty; he felt an immense sympathy for any man who might undertake to deal with *her* billion discontents.

"He's *very* busy."

Lee elected to wait. It was a large salon, densely upholstered and well supplied with yet further examples of that high-priced artist—dots and spots—who had been hoodwinking the educated world for the past half-century. Here, the magazine literature was composed of *Forbes*, page after page of smiling guillotine food. Suddenly, Lee glared up at the secretary, who looked away. At one time, he might have taken them by storm, using for that purpose his arrogance and his youth, both of which had been considerable. But not now, never again, not since he had crossed over into the fifty-second year of his age. He didn't want them.

It was 11:17 when he was at last admitted into a room that was so dark, so huge, so redolent with leather and furniture, it made his heart stand still. The man himself seemed to be in the north-northeastern corner; Lee could find him by his bald spot glowing goldenly.

"Leland, yes indeed; have a seat."

He was a manly man and affirmative in the highest degree. His handshake was affirmative too. Lee found himself seated on a low stool that just allowed him to peep out over the surface of a desk that was as dark and serene as the moon.

"How can I help?"

"Well…"

"Yes, yes? Yes?" (He was impatient—Lee had expected it. Impatience, he knew, had been recommended in the *Tao of Management*, New York's favorite book this year.)

"Well, I'm taking some vacation tomorrow, and…"

"Ummm? Right! What? Go on, go on."

"And I was wondering…"

The fellow was not listening. And now, his eyes having adjusted, Lee could see the following: first, that the man had the phone to his ear; second, that he had not one computer, but *three* (the grandest of them giving off a gastric noise); and finally (and this *did* surprise him), that there were two other men in the room, of whom one was silhouetted in the window with his hat pulled low.

"…wondering if I could have an advance, as it were. Against next month's salary."

"Advance." (He was not listening. And now, in spite of everything, Lee began to feel intimidated after all.) "Advance, you say?"

"Yes, sir. We're taking one of those cruises, you understand, and, as you might expect…"

"Yes? What's that?"

"It's expensive."

"I ween!" He was not listening. And now Lee saw with horror that he had been writing with great rapidity while at the same time running calculations on a tiny instrument that, apparently, he had not needed to look at with his actual eyes. Far away, a plaintive voice could be heard over the telephone. Lee waited. It was not just spots and dots; the man, having appropriated Hellas along with everything else, had also a gleaming white discobulus whose face likewise reflected much impatience. Lee knew this: that the man had more lief suffer major amputation than to study the Greek itself. That

was when Lee became aware of a fourth person slumped in
one of the huge leathern chairs.

"Advance."

"Yes, sir."

"Yes, yes, certainly. Anything else? Um? Alright, very
well, tell Frank I said so. Good. Anything else? What?"

"I reckon not."

The man was not listening. Lee took advantage of it to
withdraw. The bursar, who lived down the hall, never had
Lee encountered anyone so loath to depart from his money.
At last, however, he did reel off a plethora of bright green
bills that would go over very impressively in poverty-
stricken Alabama.

Valerie was absent. Lee tried, but failed, to get into her hard
drive, finding it locked—the bitch was smart. Instead he took
two cigarettes, two only, from Sidney's cache. This time, the
elevator was playing something of Shostakovich's; Lee rode
it up and down until the music finished.

Outside it was brilliant and bright, the sun's X-rays
turning the people into living skeletons. Lee moved on happily; more and more, he was learning how to speak to himself without showing lip movements. Suddenly he stopped
and then spun around, deceived into believing that one of
the sensitivity people had been assigned to follow him. What
he saw was a mile-long procession of living skeletons moving in and out of the abnormal rays.

The brokerage came up, a churchly building. He was led in
through a wooden gate and then down a paneled hallway
decorated with yet further art samples from that same
scoundrel who had won over William Street. Here, at the
very end of the corridor, there abided a sprightly little man
in opaque glasses (lenses the size of dimes), a necklace, and
a bright blue handkerchief spilling out of his sleeve. Lee knew
him well, an investment intellectual; the man hadn't shaved

in three days. At once, Lee understood that he too had been dipping into this year's Tao.

"That's right, yes, hm? Come in, come in. Very good."

"Hi. I thought I'd…"

The fellow wasn't listening. By squinting, Lee was able to see that his stock screen had dredged up in priority order all those securities most likely to benefit from the next Indo-Pakistan war.

"…thought I'd take some vacation, and so…"

"Is that right? Is that right? Well, good for you!"

"And so…" (Lee stopped. He was shocked, shocked, disappointed, and surprised that the man had called up on his monitor a large-size photograph in profile of Lee's own face.) "And so, I thought I'd liquidate some of those bonds."

The man *might* be listening. Lee waited while he made a call to someone, uttered one word only, and then put down the receiver.

"Bonds!" He seemed bemused by it. "Come now, you're not thinking of cashing in that convertible?"

Lee blushed.

"Don't even think about it, no, no, no. Not *now*, now that you've got their balls in your back pocket. Fuck 'em in the teeth! You might not get this chance again."

"But…"

"And another thing—you need to shift out of these *industrials* and crap. That's *dead* money, my friend—and put your stuff into that suntanning franchise I told you about."

"But…"

"Short the options! Put the screws to 'em! Do it!" (The monitor was scrolling. In the man's glasses, Lee could see the reflection of his own wife and what looked like a set of fingerprints moving past.) "Of course, there'll be some tax."

"Tax?" (There'd be no tax where *he* was going.)

"But don't worry, we can get a differential. After all, it's not as if you *worked* for it."

They laughed. In old times, Lee had owned a small black dog who now could be seen scrolling in the man's bifocals. His other computer appeared to have broken into a syndrome of circular reasoning, and was going through it over and over at increasing speed; never again would it be possible to use the machine for anything else, not so long as electricity endured and silicon declined to melt. Now finally, his impatience growing, the man plucked out his blue handkerchief and waved him off.

He walked five blocks, at all times conscious of the precious freight of money that he carried over his heart. This was *not* the time to fall down dead from lack of sleep and to allow the first person on the scene to file away with Judy's inheritance next to a heart that beat for someone else. Never had he touched so much money, hundreds upon hundreds of mighty bills. He felt he must travel with care, setting down one foot in front of the other, wherever the thin crust of concrete seemed to him more confidence-inducing. He was glad to arrive at his destination, a used car lot where the automobiles themselves (sorry-look-ing things!) were parked on actual soil. And so it was that at exactly three o'clock in the afternoon on a warm day in September, Lee received one of the warmest welcomes that he was ever to be given in his whole life; at once, the man took him by the lapels and then forced him, nose first, toward a little red vehicle that looked as if it had been owned by an adolescent.

"I see," said Lee. "And so you propose that a person like me, and a *thing* like that…"

The man blushed. He had a brother (Lee assumed it was a brother, judging on the basis of the gigantic moustaches that both men wore) who now quickly ran up to join them.

"Yes, I've been waiting a long time" (the brother said), "for someone like you. Volvo." (He pointed to it.)

"What?"

"Absolutely. No slightest doubt about it. A person like you? Now tell me, wouldn't you really prefer a country that knows how to stand apart from the world's great trading blocs? Country with a foreign policy of its own?"

"Well…"

"Oh Christ. *Now* what?"

"So stodgy-looking?"

"They can't help that! Look at a map sometimes. I mean it's not as if it were…"

"Shaped like Chile?" Lee roared, till he saw he was doing it alone.

"We don't sell them."

"No, no." In fact, the car did have that lovely shade of midnight blue that sorted so well with his intentions—he could imagine it turning entirely invisible at certain hours of the night. Unfortunately, the mile-meter had been turned back all to zeros.

"How old would you say this car is?"

The brother looked at him indignantly, and then suddenly slapped on his cowboy hat and turned and strode away.

"We don't ask how old *you* are."

It was Lee's turn to blush. He had one final question: "That cassette player…"

"Yes, it's a cassette player. We can stand here, you and I, and we can see that it's a cassette player. Jesus!"

"But is it keen enough to pick up background choruses and so on? For example, there's a place in *Tristan* where…"

"Now just you hold on for a goddamn minute! Jesus! That is *not*, repeat *not*, Swedish music."

Lee wanted to answer, but instead found himself being jogged back to the office where the brother sat slumped in obvious depression. There was a table spilling over with automobile parts, and next to it a filing cabinet with a cat residing in the bottom-most drawer. The last thing Lee wanted was to be offered a drink from out of one of the unclean glasses sitting about. The liquor itself proved hot, uncanny, and oversweet. The brother meanwhile had taken out a contract, a parchment with gilt running around the edges and inscribed in what looked to Lee like a variant of Turkish.

"Five hundred down. Twelve percent."

"Five hundred?"

"Even so."

"I could give you three-fifty."

"No, we have expenses." He pointed around at the office and the cat.

Lee looked at them. He did not dislike these people; it almost made him feel bad that the down payment was all they would ever see. Finally, he took out the money. There was an abundance of papers to be signed, so many indeed that he hardly noticed the struggle that had broken out over the bills.

It had been twenty years and more since he had piloted a car. He sat, dithering with the knobs, and finally then lurching out into the road and testing the brakes two or three times. The car was slow but weighty; he deemed it competent to do great damage to any person or persons who might get in his way.

The afternoon wore on slowly. From his roost, he could see all the distance to New Jersey and beyond, even unto the western sky where the sun, having worn down by now to a most imperfect form, was rotating crookedly. Already he had emptied out his desk (sixteen books and one stolen letter opener) and was waiting tediously for what he expected to be the culminating event of his whole insurance career.

She did come, Lee was the first to see her, and what he saw thrilled him to the soul. Sidney was appalled.

"Val!"

Others gathered around.

"Oh God!" said Lee. "Broken jaw! Nothing could be more painful."

She slumped into the chair.

"What happened, Val, and why do you look like that?"

"Why does she look like that? Why does she look like that? Well, how would *you* look if someone had broken *your* jaw?"

"Oh, shut up Lee. It's not her jaw, for pity's sake."

Lee came nearer, testing the girl's mandible with his index finger. Indeed, he saw no blood anywhere, neither did he see bone fragments, nor any sign whatsoever that the thing was out of kilter.

"He took my purse."

"Purse? Goddamn it, I'll kill him! Outrageous!"

"Oh, shut up Lee."

Others came. Soon enough, the chieftains from the thirty-seventh floor would be arriving to offer their commiserations as well. Yes, no doubt it would be good for her career. He did not care to stay and see it.

His own apartment was also in confusion; he did so hate to see his things uprooted from their ancient places and brought out into the light. The woman was bustling, more excited than he had seen her in years. He watched as she took up an album of music, stroked it tenderly, and tenderly lay it away in the box.

"Well," he said (speaking abruptly and startling her in the way that he so loved to do), "I did it: bought a car."

"You did not."

"Come see!"

He nudged her outside and then into the elevator where, however, someone had recently vomited. They endured it, all the way down to the seventeenth floor where a big woman started to come on board, but then changed her mind when she saw how the cable had stretched, and how the lift halted at two inches below floor level. The car itself was where he had left it, a few inches north and slightly to the east of one from Germany. Judy went forward timidly, and touched it.

"Notice how it's already well-nigh invisible, as night comes on."

"Good grief. Alright, what did you pay for it?"

"Cassette player too."

They entered, the woman sitting at the wheel. She was too short to be a driver, and in fact wanted nothing to do

with it. A spool of "music" had been left in the player, and
when he tried to take it out, the stuff became ensnared in the
mechanism. He cursed, fumed, and fought with it, finally
biting it in twain with his teeth, where it left a bitter taste.
He needed five minutes of silence before his heart could
settle. Finally:

"What will happen to us Lee?"

"I don't know. First, we have to *get* there. And then
secondly..."

"How will we live?"

"Well! We have all this money. No, this is a huge amount,
for Alabama. And then secondly..."

She waited.

"Anyway, a few years from now and nothing will matter anyway."

"Because of what Spengler said?"

"Right."

She thought about it. "But what will happen to *us*? You
and me?"

"Well!"

"I mean in *reality*."

"I don't know. A long slow deterioration, I suppose.
Things might even get better, at least for a time."

"And then what?"

"Then worse again."

"Worse. Well, how much worse can it get!"

"I don't know. In the first instance, even the plants and
animals might be affected. And then secondly..."

"Dogs too?"

"Oh certainly. They're already a good deal worse than
when I was young. Why, I can remember when..." He
stopped. The rain, which had been threatening all day, it now
set up a sudden (but also very delicious) patter upon the
metal roof. In the building, he could see where a numerous
family had gathered for warmth about the television, six
ignorant heads with spoons jutting out.

They gave three hours to the packing, and then another (with candlelight) to their last New York meal. The woman owned all manner of things, pots and pans and trash, all of which she wanted to save. The music was hers too, and only she knew how to pack it aright. Lee knew how to box the books, which is to say with ample wadding, lest they end up rubbing continuously while on the trip.

He owned thirty titles from the Loeb Series, tasty rascals that he lifted with care, sometimes even cracking open one or another of them and checking a paragraph or map before bundling up the total in one big parcel of wisdom and charm. And then too, he had his *Book of Hermits*, five volumes of some of the most dangerous writings in his whole collection. Of archeological reports, of monographs on various topics, of novels, biography, and travel, of paleontology, his treatise on the Boeotian coinage, etc., etc., etc.—more than the car could hold. What he wanted really, of course, was a new-world enzyme of some sort that might convey all this wisdom and beauty directly to the knowledge centers of the brain itself, and so dispose of all need for books, money, cars, life, and stealing.

He rose finally and went to check on Judy. He was lazy, always had been, and if they were ever to get packed, if would be *her* doing and not his own. The rain meanwhile had turned grey and noisy, and was falling in such fashion that, it seemed to him, the building must soon be eroded down to a nub, like unto that column of Lot's wife still sometimes shown to tourists.

He prepared himself a drink. Over the years, he had acquired a number of things, including the little silver revolver that he had almost forgotten about. The gun was accompanied by cleaning equipment, also some two dozen .32 caliber cartridges running about freely within the box. He had a clarinet (moss growing on the pads and mildew on the keys), also a flashlight in working order that he secreted away along with the pistol. In the drawer, he found an ancient coupon (worth a tube of toothpaste) that Judy had filled out very conscientiously but then had forgotten to mail. She had been trying for prizes, each near-success leading on to greater and greater efforts that continued over into the next drawer. It was there he found a fine yellow spider abiding in an empty perfume bottle, a dream location for a creature with manifold eyes; they looked at each other.

Time was fleeing. Quickly, Lee filled the chest with blankets and tools and medicines, and then pushed it out to the elevator. The last thing he wanted was for some other tenant to hop on board with him and spot the pistol in his belt. Outside it was black, the car invisible in truth. In his whole life, he had had but two successes—his wife, and now this car; with it, he could fly away home. In medieval times, one would have needed months to go as far as Alabama, whereas he planned to do it in under a week.

It was past eleven by the time they had filled the car and gotten into their riding clothes. The woman, she could still transform herself into Helen, merely by putting on her dark purple dress and a dash of makeup. Lee looked at her, the old hunger once more leaving him stunned, with hands hanging down. However, he had set aside these ten minutes for letting her grieve in private over the odds and ends that must be left behind.

She was calm when he returned. Now at last, they gathered at the table, lit the candle, and then took out the money. He sorted it into two piles, the shorter of them comprising the more newly minted bills. He could see her looking at it worriedly.

"How much is it Lee? Tell the truth."

"Nineteen thousand and something, all of it in green American currency. More or less. Don't worry so!"

"Nineteen. And what about the certificates?"

"Judy! We're not supposed to talk about that—I thought you understood."

"And you're *sure* there's a house on that land? Look at me."

"Absolutely! Unless someone burned it down."

She still looked worried, however. Suddenly, she rose and went to her room, coming back a moment later with what appeared to be a pouch of some kind, until he saw that it was simply a disused leathern glove with rolled-up bills forced down into the thumb and fingers. He took it gratefully, a medley of fives and tens and ones, the proceeds of her coupons, bottle refunds, and the like.

"And now, shall we go up onto the roof one last time?"

Umbrella under arm and wine glass in hand, he led her forth past the immigrant's room and thence to the stairs. Not yet midnight, and already the greater part of the population had gone off to bed. Never would he understand it, this worldwide compulsion for falling unconscious the moment it turned beautiful. It *was* chilly; he could feel the woman pressing at his side.

"How far is it, Lee?"

"I don't know. Thousand miles."

"Which way?"

He pointed. There in the extreme distance, despite the smoke and the weather, he could see the vestigial Gilead smoldering on Jersey's shore. Nearer, three children had come together in one of the windows, charmed to silence by the rain. Incredibly, someone had selected this moment to scale the ziggurat; Lee could see him dangling helplessly by a thread. In a city like this, the brightest star in the great Western philistine power, there were institutions as far as the eye could reach, quantity on top of quantity, and a form of life that was not worth living. True, it was not the extinction of this country or of that, the rise and fall of tectonic plates, no; rather, it was the neglect of literature that worried him most. He had wanted a small society getting smaller, a fine world getting finer, an enthralled people burnished by the arts, and the rest could perish for all that he cared. Sooner the better!

"Wait here." He left her, running down to fetch his suit, a green affair, much discolored, that he had intended to leave behind and let starve slowly on its hook. Instead, chortling all the way, he brought it up to the edge, hesitated, and then tossed it over.

"Good grief!"

"Never, never again will you see me enshrouded in a thing like that, never. Alcibiades would have puked, to see how modern men humiliate themselves. Now just imagine how…," etc., etc. He was raving again. The woman had learned how to listen with one ear while at the same time thinking her own thoughts, which tended to be rather milder. Just now she was looking back in the general direction of "Queens," an extensive terrain, quite flat, in which the houses seemed to be bobbing up and down, threatening to float away.

"That's where we used to live," she said, pointing.

"I know. Don't think about it."

"In the '50s…"

"Forget it."

She had a strange method of turning loose one tear only, once each ten years. He saw her stop it with her finger and flick it away.

"It wasn't always like this."

"I know, I know." Finally, he had to interpose himself between her and the view. A wind was up. And then, too, they must hurry before the watchman slammed the gate.

He drove slowly, suspicious of the puddles. In front, the ziggurat loomed up, awing both of them to silence. Two faint lamps indicated where even now the night workers were putting in extra hours with their trowels and spackling paste. The original intentions had perhaps been good; nevertheless, they would not (and *could* not) build a building two miles high. But mostly, he was intrigued by the peculiar "honey-comb" structure of the upper stories, where some numbers of the poor had taken refuge from the rain.

The river was high. They crossed haltingly, Lee at all times on the lookout for erosion, or any other possible failings in the integrity of the bridge, which indeed was heavy-laden. As for the *swaying* that they both felt... He assumed the engineers had provided for it. Manhattan itself (and this did surprise him) was in full activity; he found it swarming with men and women in suits. They passed a display window in which several nude dancers were performing wildly, but with almost no one bothering to watch. Lee pushed forward, halting when he came to a blockade of well-dressed people who had formed up into a line that, apparently, extended for a good quarter-mile into the dark regions about Second Street. Tonight, they were turbulent. He saw where two of the women, both wearing the wind-blown hairstyle preferred by the entrepreneurial class, had actually gotten down onto the pavement and were ripping at each other. Behind him, meanwhile, Lee had also noticed how the same identical Mercedes that had been following him for the past ten minutes had now pulled up even nearer and was sniffing, as it were, at his rear bumper. He could go neither forward nor backward. And that was when he realized that someone, a twelve- or perhaps thirteen-year-old boy in a black suit and conservative tie, was tapping politely at the pane.

"Yes?" said Lee. (His right hand reached for, and found, the loaded revolver.)

"Parameters of Assertiveness Extrapolation. Two?"

"What?"

"Parameters of Assertiveness Extrapolation."

Lee looked at him. Somehow, he could not assimilate what it was precisely that the boy wanted of him.

"I don't..."

"Management seminar! 'Parameters of Assertiveness Extrapolation.' You've still got a few minutes, if you hurry. Two?" (Already he had peeled off the tickets and was offering them with some impatience.)

"No, thanks."

"There's still time!"

"No. No, thanks."

The boy came nearer, squinting in at the two of them as though they were insane.

"I'm talking the real stuff!"

"No, thanks." Lee edged forward. In front, the crowd was pressing in closer and seemed likely now to break into the auditorium by sheer force. The boy, meanwhile, was standing with an expression so shocked and so pale that Lee felt responsible for having done a cruelty to him. The man in the Mercedes, *he* at least was buying a number of tickets.

After half an hour, they reached the western slum and began the dangerous voyage with lights low and all doors locked. Two drunks he saw, one of them vomiting up against the wall. Suddenly, they heard a crashing sound, someone having apparently tossed down something onto their roof from the upper stories.

The tunnel—or "tube," so-called—was free, apart from the wreck (still smoldering) that had been swept up neatly and pushed to one side. Here, the smell was primarily of sulfates and chlorides, though with some little hint of halogens as well. Ahead was the gate and, just as he had always foreseen, the gloomy-looking tollkeeper in his cape and cap. After so many years, Lee had no intention of being shut up inside at *this* date, not now, not even if it were only a tiny coin that the man wanted. The car, too, it seemed to be of the same mind. They slowed deceptively (Lee smiling broadly) and then suddenly bolted, breaking through the barrier and leaving the man in a state of bewilderment with his hand sticking out. In front, things looked different; Lee could feel an excitement coming on.

PART
II

Chapter Five

THUS LEE, AND THUS LEE'S WIFE—THEY HAD BROKEN THROUGH THAT MEMBRANE THAT HAD CLOSED THEM OFF FOR SO MANY YEARS FROM THE OUTSIDE WORLD. Possibly, he fainted; in any case, he recognized soon enough that there *were* trees, gnarled and twisted things silhouetted horribly against an ill-augured sky, and that the car knew how to weave between them in total silence, ten miles outside of New York City. That was when he slowed and stopped, not wishing to stress the car so early in the trip.

"Let us take a walk, you and I," he said. (In fact, he had to pull her out. It was far, far past her usual sleeping time.) Above, the moon was unambiguously yellow; he felt he was almost as much as in Alabama again. Other things, the cities of New Jersey, could be seen west and south, also the abominable Philadelphia in all its size—these sat on the tableland, poised like malevolent pieces in a game of chess. As to how he was supposed to get past all this, how worm his way amongst and between them—he was not at all so sure. Here nearer at hand, he saw a beer can sparkling gorgeously beside the roadbed. But the car itself—and this pleased him greatly—was very nearly invisible in darkness like this.

"Well. We did it!"

They flew into each other's arms. She was short and possibly getting shorter, but that this *was* the same woman as of thirty years ago, he could verify it by a thousand little clues. Tonight, she was in dark colors.

"Want to go back?"

"No! Heavens. Do you?"

"Absolutely not!"

"Me neither." Then: "Oh! what's *that*?"

"Philadelphia."

"And that?"

"Dilt's Corner."

She looked at it, the smallest of the chess pieces. Lee reckoned it as only some four hundred yards from the highway.

"We could live in Dilt's Corner."

"No, no, no." Suddenly that moment, the glow from Trenton (he believed it to be Trenton) weakened, hesitated, and then came back up in sparks and spumes that gave away the location of the…

"Steel mills," said Lee. "I've read of this." Never had he been in a better position to see so much beauty and so much evil, all within 80 degrees or less. An airplane passed overhead, its eye beams raking across the clouds in a non-coördinated fashion (one eye looking down). From somewhere, a frog was intoning in the heartrending woe so characteristic of the species. It warned them not to linger here.

They ran for the car, almost dashing past it in the night. Lately, he never entered a car or a room without immediately locking each door and then checking it twice. Itself, with its nose pointing in the right direction, the car seemed impatient to be up and gone and running, a healthy attitude that boded well for the miles to come. Suddenly Lee grabbed for the money, finding it all intact. The money was there; moreover, they had a pistol, two days of food, ten gallons of spare fuel, and 240 volumes of books that also functioned in lieu of ballast.

They went forward cautiously, allowing themselves to be passed by anyone who wanted. First there came a woman in a DeSoto, she too apparently fleeing from New York. She was making good speed, and yet Lee was able to catch the expression of wild anxiety in her face.

They had passed into a region that was dense with road-side signs bearing symbols upon them. Unfortunately, Lee had lost the science of interpreting them. To him it was enough that the road was open, the traffic small, the pathway clear. Above, the grand moon was now riding mile for mile with them and laughing in its belly. Lee fumbled for the brandy and then, with Judy watching worriedly, took a good long swig. Pills and medicines he no longer needed, not with New York sinking down slowly behind him in bogs and fumes. In front, an intrepid little creature of some description, a raccoon he guessed, put one foot out onto the pavement and then turned to fire back at them with amber rays. Beautiful was it, these last days as a four-thousand-year-old civilization was wobbling down to its end; even the rubbish had a glitter. Suddenly, he realized that he was off the road again, again moving too slowly. He drank. The clouds were peculiar, too layered and too schematic; to his mind they resembled, in part, the Mayan writing system, while in other parts the message looked like pure gibberish. If only he could but read it aright! For it was here that the future was revealed, in clouds alone, and never in the viscera of sacrificed heifers or, as certain old-world wizards had liked to pretend, in the configuration of camel manure.

They slowed and then ran over a perforated iron bridge half eaten away by worms. Ahead, someone was hiking merrily with staff and knapsack...until the headlights hit him. At once he ran down into the field and hid among the weeds. They were not so terribly far from the city, and yet they were constantly coming upon cows, pious creatures who sat looking intently at that place in the sky where the sun was most likely to make its next appearance. It was when Lee lowered his window—nothing surprised him anymore—that he learned they had joined together in a hymn. And whatever *he* saw, Judy saw it too. For despite the hour, her eyes were wide.

They were perhaps thirty miles into Pennsylvania when suddenly a shopping center came up out of nowhere. He had a glimpse of hundreds of youths loitering listlessly, their mouths dangling open in the late-twentieth-century fashion as they stared hungrily at the goods, and at each other. Lee put on speed. They had come into the midst of a brilliantly illuminated resort area guarded over by papier-mâché elephants (enormous things, three stories tall), together with an equal number of very lovable dinosaurs (taller yet), facing back from across the highway. He could just imagine the paleontologists of the future explaining *this*. And already the thing called Philadelphia was coming up fast and no way to avoid it, unless he were willing to try New Jersey again. Lee cursed. The radio was bad, the "music" worthless, the announcers snide. He sought desperately to dial in the weather report with one hand while with the other he tried to turn the car around. And now, for as long as he lived, never would he see the town called "Gwynedd." It had passed him in the night. Instead, Trenton came up, or rather a long-distance view of it (palpitating, greenish in hue). He detested having to backtrack in this fashion, all the way to Dilt's Corner again. Suddenly a voice on the radio began speaking in hushed tones, telling of how a certain famous football coach had just that day signed a famous contract. Lee turned the volume up. The business news was good. And if last week consumables had been doing poorly, *this* week they were registering a manifold rebound. Lee narrowed in on the station, hoping to hear the weather before they outran the radio signals. Things were good, he heard, in Oregon, a happy people enjoying their mountain fastnesses. But meanwhile snow squalls (dangerous to safety) were arriving *somewhere*, though as to *where*where…he didn't hear. Truth was, these descriptions of the weather had come to be almost his favorite sort of listening.

They ran past Dilt's Corner at four in the morning, direct on the path back to New York. He couldn't trust his own

navigation. The map, moreover, was old, and they were re-
lying upon a car that refused to go more than forty miles per
hour. Nor was he willing to put on his music, not with New
York once again in sight, and Judy sleeping.

They came to Somerville, coasted (the town was utterly dead),
and then turned off onto highway number 206, a narrow route,
the asphalt somewhat rippled. It was gloomy here beneath the
overhanging trees; Lee saw, but did not mention, the festoons
of bats clustered in the branches. Soon enough, it all flattened
out into an empty region that was so devoid of everything, it
appeared almost as if the army of the Assyrians had lately been
campaigning in the region. This then was how perhaps Death
must seem—speed and serenity in one unending dream. Or
rather, he felt as if he were running through the loops and whorls
of some giant Mind that was itself befuddled on dreams of
speed. He did see one dim lamp half a mile deep in woods
where, he liked to believe, an old one (a refugee from the
Integrity Age) might still be holding out stubbornly in a cabin.
Meanwhile, to the east an entirely new star (new to *him*) had
flared up brightly, sparkling in regions that were cold. Lee drank.
To his certain knowledge, there was an ocean not so far away,
the briny smell of it leading him on to areas that were moist.
And that was when he saw how the woman herself had come
awake and was eating quietly of her slaw and chicken wings.
Lee looked at her, whereupon she stopped, furrowed about in
the basket, and then offered up what he trusted to be one of the
wings. It was good, too, as was everything from her hand; he
could have consumed thirty of them.

"Another?"

"Certainly."

"Coffee?"

"Oh yes."

She poured it, handing it over in her serious way. There
was something to be said about this—speeding along by
night in a sealed ship with History unfolding on both sides.

It was so much better than anything he had done in years. In the mirror, New York was going down for the third time with what looked like a school of gulls gloating over the wreckage. Now, now at last, Lee turned on the music and drank. Next to him, Judy was sitting with her hands folded in her lap, her large eyes looking forward seriously into the amazing dim. But it was Lee who first set eyes upon the gigantic tumulus pushing into view from the east, the last thing he had expected to see so early in the trip. He drank. It put him in mind of his readings. And then, too, he counted himself fortunate to have been allowed this precious view, brief as it was, of the world-famous mound heaped up in such remote times against the memory of great Hector, whom Achilles slew.

They went another hour, until the pink sun began inching up in teasing fashion, bouncing in the hills. Now once again the woman was asleep, leaving him as the sole witness and testimony still awake and active at this hour, and capable of interpreting it all. He had to gasp when he saw how the dawn sent out one exploratory beam that raced down the farmland, smiting the silo with a shaft of light. This then (so he imagined) is how it would be when a new philosophy emerges, sweeping everything before it. Suddenly—and *nothing* surprised him anymore—the thing dropped down behind the horizon again, as if by change of heart. The cows, too, they got down again onto their knees, content to wait until the actual moment.

It was 6:49 when he passed Princeton University in the semi-dark, a lordly institution that looked as if it wanted very badly to belong to the Middle Ages. That it was now the *true* sun that was coming up, and not that false business of half an hour ago...he was confident of it. Putting on his best speed, he caught up with and then passed a small brown dog who, however, to judge from the expression he was wearing, no longer remembered why he had set out in the first place. In front, a huge bus, as big as the world, was bearing down upon him; Lee needed only to make a very slight mistake in order to wake up in the anti-world with his wife at his side. Two hundred and forty-odd volumes strewn up and down the highway—he could well imagine the local journalists scratching their heads over such a sight. As to the anti-world, he continued to have a vague hunger for it, mixed with curiosity. That was when his wife came awake.

"Lee! What were you thinking just now?"

Lee said nothing.

"Want me to drive?"

"No, no; the sun-wheel's already up. See? No, we need to find a stopping place."

His plan, in fact, was to search out an opening in the woods on his left-hand side; instead, almost the next thing that came into view was a tumble-down farmhouse with a chimney that was broken and scattered. He slowed and then turned into the lane. All the windows were missing, and even the door itself was lying out in the yard. Three times he circled, finally coming to rest behind the building, well out of view from the highway.

He entered most cautiously, taking the flashlight and pistol with him. The place was empty, save for a few broken bales of straw and a certain amount of debris. The roof, most of it, was missing, and he could look up directly into the trembling sun itself, there where it seemed to be having some difficulty in climbing the sky. As to the people, they had evacuated the place in haste, to judge by the message scrawled so tremblingly on the wall, with all its misspellings.

Lee went back for his wife, but only to find her sitting stubbornly, arms folded. He had to cajole with her before she would set foot in the place. And yet... And yet... Hers was a strange nature—hardly had she come inside before she began eyeing it appreciatively, even (it seemed to him) measuring it mentally for curtains.

"No, no," said Lee. "No, this is not Alabama, not *yet*." He laughed, but she did not.

70   Tired as he was, he had only energy enough to fetch in the blankets, two books, and what was left of the wings. Upstairs—and this delighted him out of all proportion— were some twenty bales of hay in mint condition. He pushed them together to form a "bed" and then spread both blankets, devoting several minutes to the job in his usual fastidious manner. The third blanket, the best of the lot, he fixed to the window, thus blocking out the sun. He was *so* tired, so utterly so, he found himself locked in a deadly struggle in taking off his shoes. And although the wings were cold and the slaw rancid, nevertheless he wolfed it all down quickly, using his fingers for tongs. Judy his wife was down below looking into the cupboards; daylight was *her* element, even as night was his. He simply had to trust to it that she would be safe in his short absence.

Chapter Six

HE DREAMT A DREAM HE HAD DRUMPT BEFORE——OF A HUMAN FACE STARING BACK AT HIM BELLIGERENTLY, HOUR AFTER HOUR, FROM TWO INCHES AWAY. Nothing could be more horrible. Indeed they were breathing upon each other, adding to the uncomfortableness of the thing. They did try to look past each other, but unfortunately, there was nothing to be seen apart from that blue "wash" that, apparently, forms the backdrop to all such disembodied heads. Lee was certain of this much, namely that somewhere the owner of this particular face was dreaming too, and no doubt was as uncomfortable as himself.

Lee was glad to come awake. At once he scrambled for pencil and paper, intending to make a description of it. Too late! By the time he finally got a pencil in his hand—it never failed—the dream had seeped away out of mind and memory.

Outside, the weather was calm and brilliant to a degree; he leapt to the window and stood gazing out over a tawny landscape in which the grasses, insofar as they pointed in any particular direction, were pointing to the South. And yet here, too, he could see the early encroachments of one of the cities, very possibly Trenton itself, reaching into Pennsylvania with tentacles composed of modern homes. Moreover, something had come into the room while he was unconscious and not only had decamped with the chicken bones but had taken one of his shoes as well.

He went down and peeped into each of the rooms. Through the ruined ceiling, many little sunbeams broke across his path, each filled to overflowing with dust and atoms that trembled in front of his eyes. Lee studied it, even inserting his hand into the stuff and experiencing the strange bombardment that had started out ten billion years before on long travels from... Oh, the things that it had seen! The places! That was when he realized the woman herself was gone.

Outside, a clutter of blackbirds harkened to him and began hooting, their fingers strangling the branches of an already denuded tree. Autumn was coming, no slightest doubt, autumn itself with its famous red leaves and notorious smells; one whiff of it and he would be in gravest danger of bursting into tears. And when he looked up, the sun-wheel had aged and seemed smaller than it ought, weaker, further, a mere red seed. In the other direction, there was a scene of yellow weeds very much like wheat itself. For he had come to the point where beauty made him turn to thoughts of music and the arts, instead of the other way around. Today, he had been set down in a Flemish landscape with crows and the sound of a wedding in the dale, and now he need only to push forward to the edge of the canvas where, very likely, Judy would be found dancing and skipping with the peasants. But first, a patch of corn (five acres worth, unharvested) that lapped the hill—it was here he found his shoe, badly gnawed indeed.

He went on, cutting through a line of beeches. In this region, the artist had used brush strokes of a thickness, even to heaping up the paint gratuitously in a dense ochre that made the corn look burnt. Each breeze set the stalks to talking. But most devastating of all was the far distant sound of a horn beckoning in the hills. All his life he had wanted it like this—one perfect moment between summer and autumn, and then, next, to extend it to perpetuity.

He followed the trail, a meandering track that led in a somewhat drunken fashion to the top of a rising where he stopped and marveled and, with the beauty of it making it difficult to breathe, exclaimed out loud. Barns and fields, sky and the open-mouthed sun—once again he felt as though it must signify something, theory made manifest, or rather, that it was a picture of the kaleidoscopic human soul itself in one of its states. Or perhaps…or rather… In short, he wasn't sure. Of course, he had to hold up one hand, if he hoped to block out the disturbing vision of Philadelphia on the horizon, a cake of brown excrement seething with worms. There were other things as well, monstrous growths in process of linking hands across the whole landscape, ignorance on top of ignorance on top of shallowness on top of noise on top of… He thought for a moment that he might actually vomit. Nor did he dare to look behind him, there where "Trenton" sat vilifying with its existence the once-lovely earth; instead, he suddenly brought up his other hand and, by force of concentration, was able to persuade himself that the 20 degrees of beauty still remaining might once more, in days to come, represent the full whole actuality of things.

The corn, he learned, was infested with grasshoppers, an incomprehensible species that looked back at him with faces that showed no slightest flicker of expression. They made him nervous, as did also a sleepy-looking lizard, ener-vated by sun and light; never had Lee seen eyes so heavily lidded, nor ribs so delicate as his. No doubt these creatures had been sent forth to spy upon human mortals.

"Where's Judy?" Lee asked. "I'm talking to you!" Then, more politely: "I know she went this way."

No answer. There were omens in the hills and omens in the corn, but he was no closer to interpreting them than when he had tried (and failed) as a boy in far-away Alabama. The lizard had gone to sleep. Foolishly, he had left the pistol in the car. Suddenly, the sun gave a quick violent shudder, turned dark for an instant, and then came back on more brightly than before—was he the only one to have noticed it? It warned of cold weather coming in. Why then was he still lingering in the northern states?

He hurried. That his wife had passed this way, he knew it for a certainty when he came to the three stones and the two sticks arranged in a certain way in the path. For they had numerous signals between them, including his special summons for when she was lost in department stores. He tried it now:

"Caw!" And then, after waiting a moment: "Caw! Caw!"

A thousand grasshoppers shifted restlessly, but Judy did not appear. Below, he could see the red tile roofs that blended so well with the burnt leaves of September, and now the buildings themselves began to come into view.

"Yes" (he said), "these are uninhabited homes, I'll warrant, with red tile roofs. But what's that 'music,' and how is it that at least one of the chimneys seems to be emitting faint traces of random smoke? It's only September."

He went on, traveling on tiptoes. The "music," it came out of a flute and seemed to be the work of someone who was far from having mastered his instrument. And now, although he had been behaving with the greatest caution, nevertheless a great burly dog had come out to join him. The dog barked, the music stopped, Lee stepped into view, blushed, and grinned.

What he saw was a celebration of some kind—twenty peasants or somewhat more, all of them in their finery. The bride (he assumed it was a bride) was a fair-enough-looking girl, her hair full of roses, while as for the boy, he appeared to be someone who knew how to hew and to plow, and Lee wanted no argument with him whatsoever. But all this was nothing, a mere routine feast so far as Lee was concerned, except for the presence of Judy, who, apparently, had *been dancing with the peasants*. Lee went to her.

"What in the…!"

"Ssssh. Be nice."

"But…!"

"Want to dance? They don't mind."

"No I don't want to dance! Goddamn it, I…" (He realized that two of the men were looking at him.) Again, he grinned, and then turned and bowed sweepingly in their direction. He had no pistol with him, in fact nothing but the nineteen thousand dollars which he was absolutely resolved to retain. That he had come forth into the country imbrued still with the smell of the city on him, the dog knew it. Lee got down to pat the thing, a mistake that gave Judy her chance—and today *nothing* was surprising—her chance to get back into the dance.

"Goddamn it!"

That was when one of the men came up. Lee had no explanation for why the fellow was carrying an ax with him. Lee smiled, nodded, and then, in his effort to offer a cigarette to the person, pulled out by error a hundred dollar bill.

"Wedding!" said Lee. "Ah yes indeed, a wedding in the woods. Peasants! Nothing surprises me, not anymore. And especially not today!" He laughed uproariously, meanwhile doing his best to get the hundred dollar bill back where it rightly belonged. "Yep, that's my wife. Dancing. I don't know why."

Now finally the man did speak. And although Lee was looking squarely into his face, and although he was but centimeters away, yet he could understand none of it. Quickly he changed into the more powerful of his two pair of glasses, as if *that* might be of help.

"Sorry, I didn't quite make out…"

Again the man spoke, this time doing it louder and closer, and giving signs that he had no great patience. Again Lee understood nothing.

"Brooklyn," said Lee. "I finally did get to the point where I could understand *them*. But in your case… Well! I have to admit it, I simply…"

Instead, the man turned on his heel and, dragging the ax after him, shambled away. It was a small brown woman, some eighty years into her age (as Lee estimated it), who now came running up to offer him a beer, or "ale" of some kind, a full quart of it in an earthen tankard with a picture of the sun and stars painted crudely on one side. Lee thanked her graciously, but then had to wait while she instructed him with gestures as how to lift it and how to drink it down. He whom nothing surprised, in fact he was greatly surprised to see, first, how the groom had his hand deep, deep into the bride's smock, and then secondly, how she was smiling at it, and thirdly, how the others were cheering him on. And all this time, the little brown woman insisted that he drink, even at one point tilting the tankard higher with a little stick that she seemed to carry for that purpose. Not that he was unwilling— it was a good beer, viscous and sweet to an extent. Now Judy came running up, very much out of breath.

"Good," said Lee. "Good, good. Ready to go back? Now if you'll just kindly put your shoes on…"

"I'm not ready."

"Jesus."

"They haven't…"

"Consummated it?"

"It won't take long. Please?"

"God Almighty. Great God Almighty, we stand here, miles away from our destination, winter coming in, and meanwhile *you*…" He was distracted by the tumult and the cheering. No doubt about it, it was a heroic bridegroom, able so easily to lift the girl, roses and all, and go running with her into one of the red-tiled homes. Two others tried to go with him, all in vain; the boy ejected them with a kick. The flutist meanwhile, he had begun playing a somewhat different sort of music. Across the way, Lee saw three men conferring, and saw further that they were all three looking back at *him*. He rather wished the little brown woman would go away; instead, she continued to pour out the ale.

"Those three men… One of them is coming this way."

"I know," said Judy. "Try to be nice."

Indeed, the person came and stood before him. Lee had seen this type before—burly, sullen, serious. Lee screwed up his ear in hopes this time of understanding the local language.

And then, too, there was a squealing (but not of pain!) that continued to come from the marriage chamber.

"He wants a hundred dollars," said Judy.

"What!"

"Hundred. For the ale."

Lee cursed. The flute player had gone off into a rhapsody, and meanwhile the farmers themselves had broken out into a wild applause that, to judge from the confirmation within (sighs and screams), was not unmerited.

He walked back in a glum mood, poorer by much. Judy, on the other hand, was still humming, still barefooted, still… That was when he noticed for the first time that she was carrying her socks in her hand, and that both were filled out like little pouches that were full of something.

"And what, may I ask, are you carrying in those socks? Hmm?"

"Corn!"

"Good, good."

"And I've been thinking—maybe we ought to stay right here."

He thought, at first, that he had not heard correctly.

"We have a house, we have neighbors, we have…"

"Absolutely not! Never. Does this look like Alabama to you? As to the 'house,' it has no roof! And do you have *any* notion of what winter would do to us in a place like this? Hum, humm?"

She reflected on it, giving heed to him. He went on:

"Now your best job at this juncture is to empty out all that 'corn,' so-called, and put your socks back on, because…"

"We need it!"

"…because it's far too late in the year to be going barefooted."

"Poo."

"You can go barefooted in Alabama."

"Oh sure. You say that *now*."

78

Lee looked at her. She had something in her that had exasperated, and had charmed, and had fascinated him every day since that first day on which he had originally set eyes on her. She was short, had a dark voice and a high, luminous forehead. Just now, she was standing in front of him, challenging him, as it were, with two heavy socks puffed out with kernels of corn. Suddenly, he grabbed for her and began tickling until she flailed and sputtered and fought, shrieking with indignation and laughter. Perhaps if she were not so very short, her eyes not so wide, voice not quite so deep, perhaps *then* he had not been so tempted at all times to seize her up and put her down, and lie next to her so much.

"What's going to happen to us Lee?"

"I don't know."

"You always say that."

"I always don't know."

The moon that night was stagnant and low; looking closely, he could very definitely see rotten places on it where, here too, late modern decadence was eating at what once had been his own special star. Thus from his attic, he spent ten minutes gazing up through the shattered roof, his mind ranging effortlessly over the entire expanse of Time and Knowledge. Others too were doing the same from other planets—for a long time he had known it—and all of them were hankering, like himself, to go leaping from sphere to sphere.

He went down quietly and spied in upon the woman, who, to his shock, had built up a considerable fire and was standing authoritatively in front of it with apron on and long-stemmed ladle in one hand. Another few hours and she would have homesteaded too thoroughly ever to be persuaded to depart.

"What…?"

"Onions! You can pull them right out of the ground!"

"Ho!"

"And carrots too!"

He came, looked, marveled, and then stepped outside—but traveled no more than a dozen yards before the crows began jibing at him again. Down along the highway, the cars and trucks were coming and going at high speed, an entrancing sight whenever the distant lightning provided a momentary silhouette of the actual drivers. One, he saw, was a vulpine man, determined looking in the extreme; very anxious was he, apparently, to get himself from where he was coming in order to reach the place where he was going. But all that was as nothing when compared to what Lee saw next.

At first, it intrigued him, and then, as the moments went by, it caused him to get to his feet and begin edging back to the cabin. No further doubt—one of the vehicles had left the highway and seemed actually to be heading straight toward him across the open field itself. He snorted bemusedly at first, then shrugged, then, suddenly, ran to fetch the pistol.

"Someone's coming! Someone!"

She blenched.

"Get out of sight! There! There!"

On this occasion, she obeyed beautifully; the last he saw, she was flying around the corner with her shirttail hanging out. Lee now waited, first in one position and then in another, deliberating with himself as to whether his forty-year-old bullets still had strength remaining in them. The vehicle itself continued to come on slowly, trundling across the ruts with what appeared to be a lantern swinging wildly in the rafters of what seemed to be an old-fashioned wagon that was itself being drawn on by—Lee could scarce believe his eyes—a despondent-looking mule. This mule, Lee now saw, was gasping and heaving, the result of having had to keep up with the motorized traffic. They parked, two men climbing down slowly, followed by a boy in a baseball cap. The cabin had no door; the three of them simply came and stood (and rather shyly too) in the empty space itself.

"Howdy."

Lee nodded.

"Looks like it's going to be a wet one."

"Nothing surprises me, not anymore."

"Had two inches, over to Camden County."

"Two! Ah, so."

"That's what they tell me. Me, I didn't see it myself." He wore galoshes, and what looked like parts of a soiled tuxedo. The boy meanwhile had come inside and was inspecting the gear.

"Yep, looks like a wet one alright. Lord, we can use it!"

"Lord!" said Lee. Then: "Winter's coming in."

(The boy had uncovered Judy's things, and now was probing about in the dark rooms, looking for the woman.)

"Been cooking, am I right? Cooking *food*. Why, I'll bet you got all kinds of good stuff in that ole pot, all kinds!"

"Oh, hardly that!" Here Lee laughed cheerfully, but then also took out the pistol and let it dangle in full view.

"Hell, we ain't going to hurt you. Don't have any extra, do you?" (He nodded toward the pot.)

Lee thought about it, stroking his chin. That was when Judy came out, both men now quickly taking off their hats in a show of respect.

"Very well," she said, "you can have some. But you have to *promise* to leave when you're finished."

"Yes, ma'am. It *is* our house however." At once, he went up straightway and, sleeves and all, began probing about in the boiling stew, searching without haste for the best thing he could find.

"Christ!" (Lee said.)

The boy, he was to get nothing, that much was obvious.

"We have carrots."

"No, ma'am; those aren't carrots. I'd get rid of them, if I was you."

Already they were backing off, the two men bowing obsequiously. Only now did it come to Lee that he had failed to load the gun. Apparently, the wagon was equipped with a radio; Lee could hear a sputtering static with each step the mule took. Lee waved, the boy waved back. And when he glanced behind him into the house, his wife was gazing dolefully into the kettle.

He woke three times during the night, twice in order to piss, and then finally, toward four in the morning, to find that he was sick. At first, he accused the "carrots," until he remembered that it had always been his habit to fall ill each time he embarked upon a transition of any importance. Adding to his unhappiness, the bales of hay had living creatures in them, shrewd ones who seemed to divine that his energy was down and his defenses weak. Thus passed the hours before dawn, a lamentable time during which he was finally able to find some distraction in a cluster of peculiarly bright stars going through a series of well-rehearsed formations.

It seemed to him the day would never come. And then, too, toward dawn, a chill came down into the valley, bringing with it the smell of frost and browned apples decaying forgottenly on the stem. He was in a race with the weather and needed to get him home again before winter fell, a difficult endeavor in his present condition, when he had not even strength enough to crawl downstairs and rouse his wife.

Pain in head, chest, heart, and mind. Lee cursed. His strength was gone, whereas with regard to his extraordinary mental development (in which he took such pride), he felt today that he was endowed with a child's silly mind. Not so silly that he couldn't write his name in the powder that covered the floor, the sun having very kindly come and made it possible to do so. He wrote more, including the opening line from Olmstead's *History of Assyria*, wherein the author tells how old was the world, even when the world already was very old. More than that he did not remember, nor could he call up any great information about Assyria itself. He could mention only two kings, and even these were but commonplace names known to millions. That was when he flopped over onto the floor and began banging for Judy.

She did come, dashing up in alarm with the pistol (which she did not know how to operate) in one hand, and with the long-stemmed ladle in the other.

"Judy!"

"I'm here."

"I'm sick, baby, sick!"

"Oh, dear." She helped put him back on the bales. "I've been expecting this."

"Sick!"

"Oh, God. Is it the heart and chest?"

"Right! Yes."

"And mind?"

He nodded. "Mind too, yes, and sun. Look at it."

"Please, Lee."

"How is a person supposed to accomplish anything with *that* goddamn filth spewing all over the place? Hm? No, I ask you!"

"Want to go back?"

"Back?"

"New York."

"Goddamn it!" He *tried* to rise, but then fell back onto the hay—the sickness was bad. His wife meantime was doing her best to fix the blanket over the window; watching her, he grew calm once again. He was pleased to have her stroke him on the back and neck, till he grew calmer still. Finally, with the headache having ameliorated somewhat, he collected the pistol from her, together with the two spare shells.

"I think I'll just…"

"Yes, dear, sleep. Sleep, sleep, and when you wake…"

"It'll be night again."

He did sleep, coming awake briefly at about 9:30 in order to rid himself of the money, which had made such a lump in his vest. He was accustomed to taking his sleep in small increments; here, far from New York, the increments were getting larger. And if here the architecture was faulty, yet he had only a twenty-foot drop, as compared to half a mile in New York.

Would the day never end? He woke again, waiting with clenched fists while the sun approached the moment of twelve o'clock, the highest point of the vaulted sky where almost at once it began tumbling "head over heels," as it were, on its long journey downhill. He was not at all surprised to see the room full of people—children and grandparents and the whole bunch of them, the shades of souls who had domiciled here in times past. A grey woman was rocking in the soul of a chair that (it too) had no doubt long ago passed through the bars of the space-time continuum and into that better Domain that had so intrigued Plato, and intrigued Lee too, or was he sleeping?

At four, his headache was worse. Furthermore, he must at all times keep his ear screwed up for Judy's call, in case she was running into trouble. And then at five, his headache improved; he was able to rise and limp to the window, there to urinate at leisure. It was a strange business indeed, the pathways of the sun; across the way, he saw four horses cavorting in the late afternoon rays, in light that was itself gilded in gold. Golden too was one of the horses, the youngest of them and the most naïve. Strange indeed were the pathways of horses. Overhead Lee now saw two crows who, devoured with envy, were aiming bombs of excrement upon the animals of the field.

Three times Judy came back to check on him; three times he pretended to be asleep. Finally, toward six, he caught the now-familiar smell of false carrots simmering in the kettle. The sun was feeble—Lee gloated over it, even to the extent of measuring his own gaze against *its*. He loved to see how it sagged and flattened, snagged on the horizon, a mere pouch as it looked to him, filled to overflowing with a fluid that had gone bad. Already the moon, or rather its precursor

84 (a ghostly presence indeed), already it had come up in the most unexpected of places and was contributing its own thin weight to help in pushing down the sun. Lee felt better now. He was standing at the window when Judy came in.

"Lee! You're supposed to be in bed."

"No, I'm better now."

"Truly?" She came forward, pressing her palm against his forehead. It was their privilege to be witnesses at the instant when the sun, valiant to the end, went down horribly in a final show of blood and gore. As if instantaneously, ten thousand lights sprang up along the highway. Lee looked for, but did not find, the grey grandmother rocking in her chair.

They packed in haste. During his sickness the woman had acquired, first, a glass jar (bright scarlet in color) that she had dug up out of the ground; second, more corn; and then finally, a curious-looking seashell that either had washed up on shore during the incredible Ordovician Age, or else been purchased from a tourist shop. All these found their way into the car, and the pistol as well. Now they moved off, slowly in the beginning, with Judy looking back regretfully.

It was gloomy along the highway, and the cars they encountered seemed to have no drivers. He was never so much at peace as when he was speeding over the world by night, the black velvet "juice" lapping at the windows; it might almost be his favorite of eras, the Merovingian centuries, when the nights were known to have endured a hundred years, and barbarians were everywhere. There had never been, nor could there ever be, any sense of security where danger is missing. Lee appreciated danger, even as the rich give thanks to poverty. Or rather, he was like that man of Florida who, in January, loved to look to Massachusetts, and to gloat.

By ten, they had passed New Egypt, a worthless hollow, largely ruinous. He saw a few loutish men dawdling in front of the tavern, as if meditating a lynching, or as if hungering for a library to put to the torch. Lee sped up. Next came miles of open country, a thin-soiled kingdom that produced a species of highly complex brambles, but not much else. He had put on his music, an orchestral suite of pure beauty in which the flutes and horns…and that was when he saw that he had *again* somehow targeted himself upon Philadelphia, the last location on earth he craved to visit at this hour. All roads pointed to it. Here, in a country like this one, the non-urban areas had come to be looked upon as simply a nuisance, a mere "fill," as it were, that hindered the cities from linking up into one contiguous nightmare. The more he thought about it, the more his gorge began to rise. He was moving well, forty miles per hour and better, far faster than ever his grandfather had traveled, and *still* it was not good enough for the other drivers, who turned and, on at least two occasions, yelled out at him. Lee reached for the pistol. And yet, the night itself was sweet; he identified the first firefly he had seen in twenty years. He spied a country youth in a straw hat and with a fishing pole over his shoulder, a twelve- or fourteen-year-old churl who appeared to imagine that it was daylight, and this the nineteenth century still. One mile further, a gas station came up. Lee slowed, looked it over, stopped.

Someone *was* inside; he could see at least three television sets glowing in three separate rooms. He tapped, courteously at first.

"Yeah?"

Brooklyn! It was a Brooklyn voice! Lee could feel his head-ache coming back. "Could I have… No! Could I *purchase* ten gallons please?"

No answer. The man was lost in instant replays. Lee waited two full minutes, and then went to pump it for himself. Astoundingly, the imbecile had left a rack of quart-sized cans of additive outside, where anyone who wanted could pilfer as many as he dared. Lee took four, tossing them hurriedly into the back of the car while at the same time keeping his eye on the profiles of the man and his wife. Inside, he saw a giant screen of the new type, showing two couples in bed. Lee took two cans more and then, courteous still, came forward and laid out the bills one by one into the man's pudgy hand, with rings on each several finger.

"How far to Harrisburg?"

Now finally the man did turn and look at him. "I wouldn't be going to Harrisburg, not if I was you."

"Oh?"

"You, you can do what you want. Right? Me, I'm telling you what *I* would do."

"Jeez!" said the man's wife. "Jeez, let him do what he wants to do, for Christ's sake! It's not for *you* to tell him what to do."

"Did I say what he could do? Did you hear me say what you could do? Did I say what he could do? Jeez!"

"Now you're *scaring* him, for Christ's sake. And he's got a woman with him too, a small one. Jeez! Let him do what he wants to do, for Christ's sake."

"I am letting him! Jeez! Do you see me not letting him? Hey! Am I not letting you, or what? You don't talk so much, is that what it is?"

"Let him go to Harrisburg, if that's what he wants. I mean, how else is he going to *learn*, for Christ's sake? Anyway, that old thing of Tony's won't get 'em that far anyway."

"What's wrong with…?"

"Harrisburg? Something's got to be wrong with it? Did I say something was wrong with it?"

"It's not *Harrisburg*, for Pete's sake. It's…"

"College kids."

"Ah!"

"Right. Drinking, you understand."

"Let *me* tell it, OK? Jeez. It was a bunch of college kids."

"Ah ha."

"Got their hands on a *racist*."

"Ha!"

"Hung him too."

"Christ, I thought you was going to *tell* it. Sure, they hung him. But the main thing…"

"They burned him."

"Will you listen to that? I thought *I* was going to tell it. Jeez."

"Burned him good too. As a lesson."

"Whew!" said Lee.

"A lesson for us all."

Lee nodded. His life, he now calculated, would be worthless if ever they identified his accent. Again he nodded and then, smiling cordially, edged back to the car where Judy, half-asleep, was squinting over the dashboard into the general direction of that city from which even now an evil smell had suffused the late night breeze.

One after another, the trucks and cars came up behind him, some of them blaring impatiently and then, as often as not, passing with curses or hard looks. Lee endured it; he knew something they did not, namely that he was engaged in carrying a good-sized library deep into a region that was famous for its dearth of books.

It was close to midnight when they passed a radio tower spangled with nervously blinking lights that seemed on the verge of outright panic. No doubt about it, there was something grand in being able to cut in and out of counties at high speed, through lands of danger, past towns, and then to run on somewhat more slowly when they entered the sleeping countryside itself, locked in sloth. It came upon him suddenly—the very same red clay field itself where old Aëtius had stifled the Hun. Surely, this was the time for music from the late Roman culture, if only such music had remained; instead, he put on Russian Mussorgsky. Came now Ctesiphon on the right-hand side, the huge world-famous arch framing the moon itself. Once more, he began to have the sublime feeling that he had had before—that they were traveling, not through positive geography, but rather through the imagination of some almighty Historian's vast mind. Needless to say, it was then that they began to pull into the outlying slops of the abomination called sometimes "Philadelphia," sometimes "Camden."

Never, never, never would he understand it, this yearning on the part of so many thousands to come together so closely, there to tilt up against one another for mutual support, sniffing, sucking, rubbing, eating—he wanted to puke. Here, even the fascination of evil had passed away, owing to over-exposure. Almost immediately he was able to pick out a whore who, like certain old-world anchorites of whom he had read, had the patience, apparently, of standing in one position for decades on end. Thirty years ago and such a vision might have thrilled him to the heart. But not now, now that it had come to this, that the late modern city had turned even wickedness to boredom.

These were his thoughts when a boy pulled up in his car and, with radio blaring, waited abreast of him at the traffic light. For half an hour, Lee had been waiting with growing anticipation for his opera to come to the part that he loved the best; now, instead, all that he could hear was the sound of pure idiocy flooding the intersection. Slowly he turned, looking into the face of the boy. Savagery he saw, barbarism, imbecility—also what looked like a map of the city itself etched into the boy's features. Finally, lowering the glass, Lee spoke, doing it politely in the beginning:

"Would you kindly…?"

"What?"

"Would you just kindly…?"

"Fuck you, man."

Lee thought that he might faint. And now, although the light had turned, and although other cars were beeping at them, he and the boy continued to sit and glare.

"The pistol," said Lee, whispering it hoarsely to his wife.

"No, Lee, please."

"Do it."

And she did do it, albeit with tremendous reluctance. Itself, the pistol had a marvelous heaviness to it, owing largely to the ten heavy shells that crowded the cylinders. Now, smiling and working with extreme slowness, Lee allowed the boy to see the first half-inch of the gun's nose protruding into view above the sill.

"What you got, man?"

"Gun."

"Naw."

Lee showed all 100 percent of it.

"Yi!"

The light had turned again; nevertheless, the boy leapt forward, plunging at hazard through the intersection and then merging into the traffic on the further side. Lee returned the gun to his wife, but then had to roll back the tape, experimenting with it, in order to have the opera reiterate its high part.

It took a full hour, or rather somewhat more, to get clear through Philadelphia's low part and into the southern belt of poor people and bad housing, where crowds of youths could be seen playing basketball at two o'clock in the morning. How fragile it all looked to him!—this city civilization, a population living at the whim of a plumbing system, of unemployment benefits, of electrical dysfunctions. Would they, could they, feed themselves in case of need? And did they know anything at all anymore about nature's providings? He doubted it. He saw a drunk, or possibly a corpse, folded up in the gutter, and at the same moment caught a glimpse in his rear-view mirror of one of the city's noblest buildings, higher than the sky, bathed in a creamy light.

Another hour—and he knew well that the supply of such hours, black ones, was by no means endless—before he could shake free of the stuff and get back onto a secondary road where he was at liberty to travel in tempo with the very lovely string quartet now on his machine. The night was wonderful at this time, the low purple hills shifting position with extreme slowness as he went on. And indeed, for him, night driving had always ranked only just after music and poesy among the greater arts. Judy, of course, was sleeping; the dark always rendered her quite helpless. For this was the time she did her worrying. Twice he saw her forming syllables, and on one occasion saw her lift her hand to ward away until daylight the troubles that gathered like wolves.

Lee turned down the music. He had been on this route before, he thought, aeons ago, Sargon in power. Never could he forget it—women leaping from the upper stories, the screaming and cries, and the bloody moon looking down on it all. Lee drank. A bend came up, and then a burnt structure, formerly a windmill, with two hanged men dangling from the paddles. Those days, he had himself played no small part, until treachery had laid him low. Now, suddenly, Bacton Glenlock came up out of nowhere. It pained him to see it, remembering as he did its quondam fame for women and dancing girls. The place had now been reduced to a simple market town with clay mews of the "box and stilt" design in which the people (if people there still were) had all bedded down for the night.

Soon they were back in open country and halfway to Uwahland before he perceived that the moon was faded and had a hole in it. Lee drank. Up ahead, an enormous cloud was in process of breaking up, and looked as if some god, or giant, had tossed up a puff of sand on the day the world had started. As for the mountains, never would he catch them, not so long as the foremost of them continued to run and hide behind the lastmost. Just then a covey of crows (one of them a deep scarlet) rose up in great clatter and headed off unsteadily toward that same aforementioned hole in the moon that Lee had been the first in the world to descry.

They entered Wyebrooke at high speed, at a little before one. This was a favored locale, deep-soiled, although tending toward the overly sedate; he felt, so late at night, that they were sailing into good harborage. One home indeed had a turret three stories high, a perfect bower for Judy (now sleeping) and for their joint collection of books—he was tempted to go up and try to take possession of it. So distracted was he, he very nearly ran into the town crier, a skeleton of a man with a lantern and staff who, suddenly, even as Lee approached, began bawling out the hour in a tremendous voice that made Judy shudder. Unfortunately, she had been taken by sleep while reading the map. And now the map was on the floor, but she was reading still.

After two hours of running in the mountains, the car began to suffer. Lee pulled over at an inn that appeared to be open, parked, and then began the hard task of trying to awaken his wife. It amused him always, the manner in which she started off by smiling at him in tender friendship, and only very much later actually opening her eyes.

"Lee!" She smiled. "Where…?"

"Pennsylvania."

"Penn…?"

"Right."

It satisfied her. She prepared to go back to sleep again. In fact, he had to lift her—she was short and in her middle years getting shorter—and then next had to run and catch her before she tumbled off into the valley. The inn itself was of logs and of massive size, just such a headquarters as he would have built for himself, had he had the logs and wanted size. Moreover, a sublime smoke was issuing from the chimney with a smell of venison in it. This then was what it was to be free and in mountains, and to be putting in at a tavern at a fine hour; he had the feeling that they were young again, once more setting out with all their first enthusiasm of 1957.

Inside, they found a bright yellow fire with half a deer turning on the spit. The hosteler was a thick, bustling man in peasant attire, and with a creased face that reflected no hope whatsoever; he it was who led them to a table whence they could peer over into the enormous valley squirming in a million lights. Was it Philadelphia, which he had thought to have left behind? Valley, night, fire, and the incomparable Judy grinning at him across the table; he begged for but six years more of it, years of music and Judy and then, if so be it must, an oblivion to begin at the same moment the century must end.

"Like mountains?"

She nodded vigorously in high enthusiasm.

"Someday, we'll live in mountains too."

"With our dogs?"

"Yes, yes, dogs too."

"And horses?"

She was dreaming. Of horses, their essence and true nature, she knew next to nothing. Came now the meal, the peasant having brought not only a fine meat with gravy on it but a dark beer as well. Holding it to the light, Lee thought that he could read the future in it.

Once more fleeing to the west. This was in truth the most beautiful hour of the night, *his* hour, and a promise of the time when it would be night always, and none left alive but artists and heroes, and the myriad of little gods that liked to mix in their affairs. Suddenly, the town of *Honey Brook* came up, but then dropped off behind so abruptly that he had time enough only to verify that everyone was sleeping. As to the brook itself, it *might* be of honey, as sluggish as it was, and as tendentious. But he doubted it.

The night wore on. He slashed through *White Horse* at forty miles per hour. *Intercourse* came up (he had nothing to say about it), and then next, an exceptional place called *Bird-in-Hand*. It was a mistake, however, to be using the radio in this part of the country; there was only one worthwhile station, and *it* was dedicated heart and soul, apparently, to the compositions of his least favorite of all known centuries, the eighteenth of its line. (He liked his music to be more recent than that, and his literature older.) Just then, they sliced into the town called

Unicorne, which, to him, looked like nothing so much in this world as a slightly more exotic version of *White Horse.*

But now it was only a short sprint before the next state. It gave him a wonderful feeling, that of crossing boundaries and of moving out of jurisdictions, thereby placing more and more territory between himself and New York City. Furthermore, geography had him in its pull.

Maryland appeared to be empty, apart from the two armored personnel carriers that had parked off in the pasture on the right-hand side. In front there was an enormous city, this one tinged with a pale blue light of such delicacy that it seemed to be beckoning to all the world's youth, that they should come forth out of the countryside and sign with this or that corporation and—and Lee wanted to puke—spend a few dozen years in this or that office building. He drank. He could also make out two further cities in the extreme distance, one pink and the other a lovely shade of forest green, both of them trying to hide behind each other. Holding Wagner in reserve, Lee now quickly threw on a tape of Sibelius in its stead. His disappointment with highway number 269, meanwhile, was growing. Yes, it might have been a major thoroughfare in colonial days, but now it was beginning to unravel in places. Nonetheless, Lee went on uncomplainingly for another five miles before he slowed, pulled over, halted, and then got out and explored the rough edge of the highway with the aid of his flashlight and a pencil sufficiently sturdy to plunge into a stuff that proved as yielding as flesh. There was no other traffic, none, the locals having long ago learned to distrust the engineering that had been performed on this particular route. He went on more slowly therefore, keeping the speed below twenty miles per hour. To starboard, another good-sized town came up out of the obscurity, this one blowing off an immense funnel of tumultuous smoke comprised of billions of little souls twisting in agony. Suddenly, he shot over a lagoon, berry-colored, and dark enough and deep enough to house every manner of primordial living thing, whether catalogued or not, bottom dwellers holding out stubbornly against Time, Change, and Evolution itself. He pointed to it, there where the moon had shattered into six large fragments bobbing in the current. He wanted to speak, until he realized that Judy (who had recently come awake) had crumpled off to sleep again.

He slowed and then turned onto highway number 213. Again, no traffic; his nervousness increased. A reptile slithered across in front of him, a plump creature with a toothy smile. The sea was near—something in the flora and in the quality of the night told him so. A lighthouse made its appearance, a crude structure surviving from Anglo-Saxon days. He turned onto a subsidiary road, a mere path built up out of oyster shells. Here were cottages, also a mile-long fishing net hung out to dry so long ago that it had turned into a trellis of bright red rust. The salt wind was striking him acutely; never, not for one moment, could he forget that winter was coming in. As to where precisely he had come to… He had expected the ocean to be to the *East*. Two miles off, a boat was bobbing merrily; watching it, he actually veered off momentarily onto the sand. Very sensitive was he to the near-presence of deep sea animals, a humorless race, progenitors of his, now lined up shoulder-to-shoulder in the deeps while wishing only to endure the fearsome night.

He drank and then sped up to run over the arc of a bridge. Life, earth, ocean, night, and sea—he craved to halt and rush down into its welcoming arms; instead, he went on for another several miles, drinking even while the cities went on twisting and, as it were, exchanging locations like monstrous chess pieces nudged by gods across the provinces of the earth.

So Lee found himself at five o'clock in the morning driving down a sandy hook that jutted out to sea. The surf here was not so much blue, or even green, but rather a fruity purple that, as it splintered onto shore, sounded like utterances and screams. One could learn much, if one could but listen rightly. He parked and then went around to open the door for his wife, who had been taken by sleep with her eyes still open. It still remained *his* time of day, not yet *hers*; he had to lift her in both arms, delicately. Immediately, a small white crab leapt out from underfoot and scampered off, the Devil himself in one of his minor manifestations.

He carried his wife down to shore and set her up against a piling. Across the lagoon, it was blazing with lights and traffic and what remained of the moon.

"Where are we, Lee? Be honest."

"Sleep, dear, sleep."

Suddenly, there was an eruption on the opposite coast where, he assumed, one of the cars had exploded. The sudden illumination revealed a whole vast nation of ghost crabs some fifty yards further down shore who, once having opted to move, moved with one soul. The earth trembled beneath their "feet." In such numbers, they could easily have picked to pieces both Lee and his wife, who, however, were taking care not to irritate them. That was when one of the gulls stopped suddenly in flight and then swooped down low in order to verify that it really was Lee and his wife at such an hour in the morning.

He disrobed quickly and moved out through a surf that was chillier than he would have preferred (the moon having done nothing to warm it up). Something was sniffing at his ankle. Now, taking his courage, he swam out a distance until he came to a placid zone, thin as naphtha.

Never had there been a substance (sea) as strange as this—it fled out of his hand, sparkling darkly. Suddenly he dove, racing for the bottom, a longer distance than he was prepared for. It was easy to get lost; even after he came to the surface, he was still not certain where Judy was sleeping. Already the "false dawn" had come and gone, and now was mustering for a more successful return. Lee waited for it, focusing upon the spot where he expected the thing to leap up in glory; instead, when it came, it was several thousand miles off course and had a worrying look to it (the color was all wrong) that made him question whether this were not an intruder star that had somehow become decoupled from its own proper system. Lee availed himself of its unhealthy light to dive again to the bottom and explore about with his hand, as if the ocean floor might indeed be littered with those "diamonds" mentioned in Rimbaud.

When the dawn did come, it did so in great suddenness, finding nothing of Lee but a head floating on the surface. This was the authentic sun, staggering in might and size, and full to bursting with new-churned butter. *Now* he understood why it was the ancients used to stay up for it, bursting into cheers. Judy, too, she had come to her feet and, shielding her eyes, was searching out to sea. Hcw small she was! And how great the sea. Lee drank. It was a grainy scene in which the pigments had not been ground down to perfect fineness. Again he dove, spinning in it, saying, "So much, then, for what I leave behind in the cites," and then adding: "It has nought to do with *me*." And that was when a little silver shad leapt up and looked him in the eye.

He came to shore, pulling himself by main force out of the clutches of the sea. The woman was angry.

"Alright for you! And how would *you* like it—think about it!—to wake up with…*those*" (she pointed to the herd of crabs grazing not far away), "*those* all about?"

"I wouldn't like it."

"Where are we, Lee?"

"I don't know. East Coast."

"East. And yet the ocean is in the west. And that city there?"

"Philadelphia?"

"We've already done that one!"

"Ready for a swim?"

In fact, he had to chase her. He was quite prepared to lift and transport her and, if necessary, to take her into the water fully clothed.

"No! No!"

Lee stopped. On the road, two tourists were witnessing it with high indignation, one of them a boy with a pail and shovel, and the other a pasty-looking office thrall with camera and shorts, a straw hat, umbrella, lunch, suntan oil, pot belly, etc., etc., etc.

He drove slowly, his eye at all times reserving a view of the sea. Dawn was finished, wherefore he switched over from Debussy to Ravel, doing the transfer quickly. Here the grit was seething across the road, part of that eternal migration that had been in train for as long as the earth. He saw unnatural shapes jutting a few centimeters above the sand, the tips of ancient buildings with, some of them, good workmanship in the carvings. One mile further, just as the peninsula began to converge in upon itself, he came to a gas station with no one, seemingly, on duty. This was the ideal moment to draw off a full fifteen gallons at no cost; instead, he got out and strolled around to the rear of the building where a path led off a short distance to a cottage with shutters and a red tile roof. Very definitely, someone was bending and stooping (and talking to herself) in what appeared to be a garden—a big woman in a bonnet. A face like that, and he knew he was far from New York.

Chapter Seven

"**G**OING SOUTH!"

Lee was shocked. "Why, how on earth could you know that?"

"Don't take that one, it ain't ripe yet."

It was a good harvest she was bringing in: plump squashes, peppers, pulse beans.

"Are you responsible for all this?"

"My husband."

"Ah!"

"But he died."

"Oh."

"And now I don't know what to do with it."

They lifted the basket between them and carried it to the kitchen, a bright, clean room, admirably tidy. Bottles and jars in great number were there, onions woven into ropes, also a calendar that pictured the sea, as if she couldn't get enough of its beauty merely by looking at it through the window. Beauty on top of beauty, jars on top of jars; Lee watched as she seated herself—she was a largish woman—and began to snap open the beans. Judy had come up timidly meanwhile and was spying in through the open door with worry, interest, amazement, and pretended indifference.

"New York girl?"

Lee admitted that she was. "She cannot, however, be judged upon that basis. Now that city over yonder"—he pointed—"how is it called exactly?"

"The wee one?"

"Nay, nay; the *grand* one."

"Them's two cities."

"Two!"

"The grand one, why it might be *Warshington*. Or, it might be *Baltermore*. Now if you look real close, why they's a gap in between 'em."

It was true; Lee came closer. He was able to make out a very discernible hiatus, narrow but well fenced, a sweet green sward, as it looked to him, that kept the two modern cities at elbow's length.

"But I wouldn't be going there, if I was you."

"No, no."

"Because…"

"I understand."

"…awful, awful."

"Yes."

Judy had chosen a fruit and, taking a seat in the corner, was slowly and studiously peeling the thing. She was not yet fully awake, and meanwhile Lee was turning profoundly sleepy.

"Some people," said the woman, "*like* to sleep in the daylight. 'Course now, I was always real glad my husband weren't like that."

Lee followed her back to a tiny cell, a child's room formerly, in which the model airplanes were still dangling from threads attached to the ceiling. And on the wall, a colored print showing the jolly moon smiling down with human features upon an impossibly picturesque farmscape. The bed, too, impossibly short; nevertheless, he planned to get some good sleep from it.

He woke once, stood, and then, after thinking about it and recollecting where he was, went and explored the other rooms. Outside, the sun was so bright and so blinding, and

100   the beach so extensive, so featureless, and with no hint of
where his wife was keeping herself just now... He went back
to bed.

He woke again, but the sun was still bright.

It was six o'clock, he estimated, when he woke for the last
time. The sun was there still, but smaller now, and in its old
age, turning bilious at cheek and jowl. Judy—very seldom
was it that she allowed herself to hum or sing, and seldomer
yet when he could catch her at it. She blushed. Lee noticed
that she had gotten into her apron again and was laboring at
the stove with her knife and spatula.

"She wants us to stay, Lee."

"What!"

"There's so much to be done!"

"No doubt, no doubt. I did not, however, leave New York
in order to *do* things."

Someone had done things—he saw two new-made pies, also
a bowl of horned shrimp, all of them in the praying position.

"And Alabama? Have you forgotten so soon?"

"And the roof, Lee. It needs to be repaired."

"Jesus."

"Well *she* can't do it!"

He went out, cursing. He needed only a minute to find
the ladder and then to clear away the accumulation of palm
fronds and dead gulls on top of the cottage. From this vantage,
he could see far, too far, further indeed than he wanted. The
Late Modern West, it had come to this: a two-star system
comprised of a red giant called "Warshington" and a tiny
white dwarf named "Baltermore." He scanned further,
changing finally into the stronger of his two sets of glasses.
He believed that among the intervals of haze he could also
catch glimpses of the strange, distant, high-walled
"Wilmington" as well, its six royal pennants furling gaily in
the breeze. The other direction looked down into a road, or

rather a scarcely demarked trail, too narrow for cars, that staggered on for a quarter of a mile before petering out in the dunes. Yes, this might well suffice as a locale for that new-world "monastery" he sometimes envisioned, where people of good intentions might establish that "scriptorium," or "thinking place," of which he had so often dreamt, and possibly also an aid station for refugees from the two-star system who, he assumed, would shortly enough be washing up on shore.

That night, they gathered at the table. Judy had done the cooking—there was nothing like an apron and a ladle to bring out her authoritarian side. The woman, meanwhile, sat in the corner with the hundred pieces of a disassembled carburetor in her lap.

"Judy thinks maybe you'll decide to stay right here!" (She gave a short amazed laugh at the thought of it.) "You want to? There's lots to do."

"It's kind of you, but…"

"I wouldn't be going to Alabama, not if I was you."

"Yes, well…"

"Snakes! And oh, the heat of it!"

"He *likes* heat."

"We get plenty of heat, plenty. Just wait 'til July."

"Yes, well. However, you see I own a bit of land down there, and…"

"*I* got land! More than you. And water too! *You* got water? No." (She pointed to the sparkling Chesapeake.) "And oysters? Why Lord God, those 'good ole boys' down there couldn't bear up under the kind of oysters *we* got."

That was true. Lee hesitated.

"And besides, that old Volvo of Tony's won't take you that far anyway."

Lee could feel his gorge rise slightly. "And yet, its carburetor *is* in one piece."

"And melons!"

"True." (She had a good dozen of them stacked neatly in the opposite corner.) "Melons, oysters. And vegetables too, straight from the garden; I've seen them."

"He's weakening."

"No, no." (He could not but grin.) Then: "I *will* think about it however."

Midnight found him reading, reading well, reading in volume number three of his purloined set of Grote's *Greece*. And yet, the bed was so narrow, and Judy so short... He had his work cut out for him if he hoped to turn the page without rousing his wife from her well-deserved rest. Nor was that the worst of it—as luck and fiction would have it, he had come all the way down to the last chapter (a particularly good one), in which the great historian tells about the miserable fate of the man *Histiæus*, and the things that were done to him. Lee was appalled, his anger rising against the Persians. That was when the book ended.

He tried to join his wife in sleep. Finally, his anger *not abating*, he extricated himself, dressed silently, and then, carrying the revolver and the candle with him, left the cottage and began to climb back toward the highway and his parked car. There was a fog over the moon; looking closer, he espied what appeared to him a myriad of little ships traveling at high speed in company with the clouds. He understood so little about coastal conditions. And if the sea appeared calm just now, yet it was the most specious of all forms of calmness. (He had read about the nightly butchery taking place just below that "calm" skin, wrinkled in places, that had settled over the tide.)

At first, he worked with great patience. So certain was he that he knew just where to find volume number four, so absolutely guaranteed of success... And yet, the book was not there. Lee cursed. He was able to pick out all manner of volumes, some good, some bad, and some of them even from the same set in which he had been reading. Volume number four, however, he could *not* find. And meanwhile his reading mood—his affection for the Greeks and his wrath against the Persians—the mood had pretty well drained away.

Twelve-forty-five found him sulking behind the wheel, a pistol in his lap, and next to him the candle, the wine, and volume number five. Must he indeed go through the whole balance of his life in entire ignorance of those very crucial years (the best of all known years, in his opinion) that were detailed in the missing book? He drank. Once again, the cities had exchanged positions on the further shore, with Baltimore now "hiding," as it were, behind the left shoulder of Washington's golden glow. There, too, nightly butchery, as evil as any in the sea. His feelings were mixed: half of him wanted the cities to disappear; his other half desired that the country people would themselves go in unto said cities, thereby leaving the fields and meadows to himself and his wife alone. He drank. Very inconvenient—reading by candlelight. In any case, the mood was gone. Finally, he stood and stripped off his shirt and made a bag of it for his book, bottle, and gun. The night itself was still tropical, with no hint in it that winter was gathering just on the other side of the dunes. As to the objects jutting up out of the sand, Lee went to several of them, examining each in turn by candlelight. In the cottage, the women were sleeping, while in front, for as far as he could see...

He ambled far, up to the headlands and then, following the shore, past an abandoned oystering operation with three separate mountains of extinct shells heaped up to sharp points. Here, one could read in utter quiet; unfortunately, he had to preserve what remained of his wasting candle. And in truth, the place reeked of a million deaths. He stepped past respectfully, coming out upon a long, level, flat place, moon-drenched, very like that other shore where, long ago, Hector used to divulge his secret worries on just such nights as this.

He journeyed on, drinking. Europe, too, he knew, was in decay, and he was just as glad he couldn't see that far. Nevertheless, he did climb one certain dune, taller than the

104 others, and then held his candle more or less tentatively toward England and France. The stars tonight were in an amazing array, sticky things that needed only to brush up against each other in order to adhere, forming greater and greater globules even as he used his Will upon them. This way, then, lay the famous islands of England and/or France; he could almost climb to them across a trellis made of meteors. Or, he could use the light for reading.

He was sleeping a sleep that had started out well enough, but that then turned to so many multifarious bad dreams that soon there was nothing left to him but a worm-eaten structure held together by thread alone. Lee cursed. Already he had been made to rouse himself when the tide turned, and to fire off three shots at a certain jesting crab that had grown too bold during the time that he himself was suffering under the spell of sleep. The wine bottle was empty. Finally, he forced himself to stand and stretch, and to shake the sand out of his lap. Behind him, a thousand miles to the north-northeast, winter was coming in, and with nothing between him and *it* save only a thin slice of crimson-colored autumn now encroaching ever so slowly, inch by inch, over the once-lovely terrain of ancient Pennsylvania. In fact, the wine had poured off into the sand itself, where he could by no means get at it. Again he fired, smiting the sea itself, and then immediately regretting it. (For he had not forgot what befell arrogant Xerxes, when *he* had dared to punish a body of water much like this one.) "No, no," said Lee, grinning weakly, and apologizing within himself. What could a bullet do? The sea was broad, so broad, and yet…

He ran, stumbled, picked himself up and then fled as hard as he could from what later on was to be called "the most severe storm in fifteen years." The lightning seemed to come from the city, as if the Baltimoreans, exasperated beyond all endurance with his opinions, were hurling the bolts specifically in his direction. It needed real courage for him

to stop and turn and go back, and then to scout about in the
sand for volume number five before the tide could get it.

No rain. Lee found that he could stroll straight forward
and leave the thunderbolts—twice he fired at them—to come
crashing down vainly in the place where he had been. It was
the gulf itself that presented the danger, a hooded monster
that crawled lewdly to shore and then suddenly rose up,
thirty feet high, before spilling its treasure out upon the shore.
Shells he saw, driftwood, trash, and a computer monitor with
a fractured screen. He had said there was "no rain," and
yet obviously it *was* raining both west and south, and up
to Morgan's Bend. His inclination was to wait for further
treasure, but his duty was to run to Judy's aid.

He found them shivering behind the furniture. The
woman, who was largish, was the calmer of the two; Lee was
surprised to see that she had gone to bed wearing an applica-
tion of beauty cream. Judy, Judy was *not* calm; he dashed to
her side.

"Lee!"

"I'm here."

"Let's go back!"

"No, the highway will be all torn up by now. The hail."

She burrowed into him. She was short and possibly getting shorter, and she fitted into his embrace perfectly, once
he removed the pistol from his belt.

"What's going to happen to us, Lee? I woke, but you
were not there."

"Rest, rest."

She continued to tremble however. In Baltimore, the
lightning throwers had been given a new location; Lee saw
with consternation how one of the bolts hit down not far
from where the Volvo was grazing. The big woman, she had
been through it before, Lee divined, and she had faith in the
structure of a house that had been made by her husband.

"Ah well" (said Lee loudly), "I suppose all this will blow
over soon enough!"

"Not necessarily."

"Every book I own is in that car." Then: "Possibly the time will pass more quickly if we sing or, perhaps, tell stories."

"We heard people shooting at each other too!"

"No, dear; it's only the thunder. Rest, rest." (From the window, he could see a rich harvest washing up on shore, not all of it rubbish. Among other things, he saw a good-sized dolphin who, through great exertion (together with some luck) did finally succeed in getting itself back under the dark cover of the sea. No doubt about it, the lightning was migrating ever so slowly toward the East, there where it would find only the narrowest spits of land to squander its strength upon. Now, seeing that the winds were strong but not fatal, and the thunder retreating, and dawn coming, and that it promised to be the bloodiest-looking sunrise that *he* was ever likely to witness… He could feel his old aplomb returning.

"I think I'll just… Go outside. Stroll around."

"No!"

"He's crazy, your husband. *My* husband now, he was mean, but he weren't crazy."

"Stroll around, see what I can see. Shoot, I'll come back soon."

"No, no, no! Alright, I'm coming too."

They moved in tandem, hand in hand. As to the litter, they saw heaps of it, together with scalps of seaweed, sundered crabs, here and there an amazed fish flapping on the sand. But all this was as nothing compared to the great quantity of antique coins that had been cast up, as well as ancient pottery, some of it inscribed with pornographic scenes that took the breath away. Lee went for the coins, Judy for the shells. Above, dawn made rusty noises, like the door of a long-sealed vault being opened. Inside was the sun.

"Why, we could devote the rest of our lives to sorting through this: specimens, shells, and so forth."

"I know!"

"Artifacts. That's called *Minyan Ware*; no, I've read quite a lot about it really." Then, drawing her aside, he whispered: "Coins. Do you have any notion of what Byzantine coins go for in the open market?"

"That one's got a king on it."

"Basil. He wasn't one of the worst of them, nor yet one of the better. However…" He stopped. The woman was coming up, trudging laboriously, her arms laden with stuff.

"My, my," she said. "And now I reckon we'll just have to get as much as we can while we can. Look at Baltermore."

Indeed, the city seemed smaller, lower, flatter, with many toppled buildings. In the face of such a tragedy, they all did try to wear serious expressions. Judy alone was sincere.

"My, my."

"And now soon the Baltermoreans will come crawling up on shore. Where shall we put them, hm?"

The day passed in ecstasy while they gathered up the things. And by afternoon, the sky was of an innocent eggshell blue that seemed to forbid all discussion of last night's violence. The clouds, when they came, took on the features of great men's faces. Kant he saw, and later Schopenhauer returned in glory. For himself, Lee had had enough of it, enough of collecting, enough of pots, enough of running back and forth to the Volvo with his loot. Judy too—together they drew off a distance, out of sight of the woman and the world. So beautiful a day—they felt they comprised the first man and woman.

"As if we had just emerged out of the darkness of chaos in order to set foot upon…"

"This."

They flew into each other's arms.

"And now, back in New York—assuming New York still exists—they'll be streaming down Broad Street, millions in suits."

"I know!"

Impossible not to laugh, especially so with the beach aglitter, kings peeping out of the sand. He thought he saw old Chosroes himself, a vindictive-looking scoundrel with an excessive beard on him. The sea itself was blue to a degree, and splashed around them—they were up to their necks in the stuff—joyfully. The little fishes! Apparently the storm had chased all their predators away. It was Judy they loved, not him; for her sake they were ready to roll over smilingly, and allow themselves to be taken.

"Well!" said Lee. "So. And now it's time to think about…"

"No, Lee."

"…continuing on our way."

"Please, Lee. Why can't we just stay here?"

"You say so. One might almost think that you were serious."

"I *am* serious! I am. My word, we could live here *forever*." (She pointed around at the sparkling Chesapeake, the sand and cloud faces, the litter on the beach.)

"'Forever,' she says."

"Yes! Anyway, I don't think that old car…"

"There's nothing wrong with that car, not if you have any feeling for it."

She wanted to say more; Lee, however, had been leading her deeper and deeper, till the plashing waves threatened to cut off her speech. She was short, defenseless, wide-eyed, and had the bravest spirit of any woman of the later modern West; looking at her, grinning at her, he was again overcome by his own thirty-year-old history of lust.

"I'd like to…"

"No, Lee, please. Besides, you look like a…"

"Monster?" he grinned. "I'll shave tomorrow."

But she was backpeddling as fast as she could across the wrinkled ocean floor. At one moment, he had her in his fingertips, only a moment later to lose her again. Half a mile away, he could see where a party of youths, Washingtonians

he theorized, had come down to pick and choose among the
debris. He could feel his gorge rising. The beach was *his*,
and everything on it. Several times he yelled out at them
and then, seeing that it had no effect whatsoever, fired twice,
which had a *magical* effect.

They gathered that night in the kitchen, each of them inspecting in sullen silence the objects that each had collected. Lee,
greedy always, was pouting over his coins. He had spent
much of the evening in trying to refurbish them, only to be
hugely disappointed when he found that those of Chosroes
were gilded very cheaply, a mere tincture over base metal
indeed. How now he longed for a decent Sassanian dictionary!
Suddenly, he glanced up to find the woman eyeing his things
with more interest than he liked to see.

"Tomorrow," he said, "we'll bring in the rest of it."

"Be gone, tomorrow."

"What!"

"Now if I had me one of them *coins*, just *one*, why I
wouldn't think no more about it."

"I'm sure he'll give you *one*. Lee?"

Lee hummed. He was sitting in just such a position that he
could see out over the flat level sands of the beach where, in
moonlight, the objects seemed already half-buried and sinking
fast. His greed was satisfied, but not so his lust. Numerous times
he glanced over at his wife, who moved her chair two inches
further each time. Just now she was fretting worriedly with her
buttons and starfish, and the other rubbish she had selected.

"I'd like to…"

"More pie?"

He took it. His eye was upon the wife. Finally he said this:

"Shall we go for a little walk, you and I? Me and you?"

"Yes, you two kids don't want to be cooped up all the
time. You're going to want your own house too—I don't
blame you—and I know just where we could build it." Then:
"*We* used to take long walks, my husband and me. Hell,

110   there's nobody out there."

They tiptoed far, even down unto and beyond the coastal bend where they found themselves directly beneath that same luminous moon that tonight was imprinted not with just one face, but bleachers full. Lee had not brought his pistol.

"Ah love," he said. "And so we've come to this: halfway between Alabama and New York, and *more* than halfway between birth and death."

She snuggled up to him, as if for warmth. She was short and possibly getting shorter, but was still the pretty wife whom he had captured when she was in full beauty, and when the country had been in health.

"Will you remember me, when we are both dead and spinning through space?"

"Please, Lee."

"Well tell me this—don't these sands still feel somewhat warm from the last loving couple who stood just here, a thousand years ago, the wife getting shorter? Now both are spinning through space."

She burrowed into him. The moon was clear, the faces on it assuming all sorts of various expressions, and meanwhile not so far away, the crabs were growing bolder.

"Come, love. Didn't I say that our love would last five hundred years?"

She nodded.

"And that then we'd turn into two giant mountains standing side by side through all eternity?"

"Yes."

"Well then! Take off all your clothes now, and…"

She did so, doing it slowly, languorously even, and then, as he stood hypnotized, turned and drifted down to sea, lingering long enough to look back at him ruefully, like Greek girls did.

Chapter Eight

DAY AFTER DAY, THREE FULL WEEKS OF IT, TILL HE BEGAN TO FALL INTO DESUETUDE. Not to say that he didn't sometimes do a bit of work for the woman, or read, or, preferably, stand long hours on shore and cast his line out into the region from which, in due time, winter would be coming in. Never had he enjoyed better fortune with the fish; they came to him voluntarily, it almost seemed, perfervid in their wish to discharge their earthly mission and be done with it, until at last he began to weary of the great slaughter he was bringing about. The final moment came when he hooked a bright green creature, dappled and seductive, who tried to talk to him. Thereafter, he resorted more to his books, and less to the sea.

On the twenty-second day, he brought in his whole collection of tapes and appropriated the woman's machine; in this way, he could lie on shore in the grasp of his most beloved music, Mahler and Sibelius and Ravel, beauty on top of beauty, and genius along the Chesapeake. Add to this a few good volumes of Victorian historiography, Judy, and the first true sessions of genuine sleep that he had had in twenty years... His arrogance began to take on new growth. It was worse than that—he began to imagine he possessed the whole peninsula.

The twenty-third, twenty-fourth, and twenty-fifth days he passed with Hodgkin's *Italy and Its Invaders* in his arms.

He read deeply and profoundly, sometimes also looking out to
sea where Italy itself (he liked to believe) was *still* enthralled
in the strange toils of those indescribable centuries that seemed
to speak to him directly, man-to-man, as it were. But on the
twenty-sixth day he rose and did some repairs about the cottage. It was shortly past noon that the woman came to him
timidly, bearing a steeping glass of very cold tea.

"Judy wants to stay."

Lee said nothing.

"She's going to try to talk you into staying too. Don't
tell her I said so. You want to?"

"Screwdriver. No, the other one."

However, instead of passing the tool to him, she took
his hand suddenly into her own mighty paw and then began
towing him at high speed toward the garden itself.

"All that," she said, "all the fourth part could be yours,
the tomatoes, squash, all of it."

"Melons too?"

"Yes. Yes, I know how you feel about that—Judy told
me. Or anyway, the second share of the harvest that comes
from the fourth part."

Lee looked at it. He had not seen leeks like that, so stalwart, not in twenty years. "And the leeks too?"

"No. No, the leeks you may *not* have. Sorry! All else,
yes. But of the leeks you must not taste." Again she seized
up his hand (forcing him to drop the screws) and then
marched him down to the coast at a much faster step than
was natural with him. Apparently she controlled this whole
side of the peninsula, a complete four or five hundred acres,
he judged. Most of it, of course, was waste, although he did
see at least two goodly stands of long-leaf pine.

"And now I ask you: have you *ever* seen a more fitting
site for that 'thinking place' you're always going on so about?"

Lee had to smile; it *was* an inviting spot, hedged all
around with good-smelling trees. He could imagine himself
carrying on some tremendous thinking just here, on the

leeward side over against Todd Point. Suddenly, she bundled him off again—preternaturally strong she was—nudging him forward across a broad flat shore still littered here and there with bits of jagged pottery.

"All this, west and south, even unto Perryville on the one hand and thence down to Hooper Strait and that two-hundred-year-old spreading oak, assuming it's still there."

Lee studied it critically, rubbing his whiskers. The world here was white, becalmed, and so much like death itself that he could feel a drowsiness coming on. This was not the salt Chesapeake, but rather a proton soup. Or rather, a billion agglutinated souls, the yield of all the years.

"As to Warshington, that of course does *not* lie within my gift."

"I don't want it."

They trudged back, both deep in thought. Behind them, the ocean had "turned" and, drawn on by the gravity of the moon and the two-star system, soon it would be deep even where now the shards were glistening.

"How it groans!" said Lee. "The sea. If only one could but decipher it rightly."

"I wouldn't know. My husband now, *he* was the scholar."

"Winter's coming in."

Thus Lee and thus Lee's wife, and thus the woman too... By the evening of the twenty-eighth day, the cottage was in good repair, and all three of them were gathered in the kitchen, where they refused to look at one another. The woman was sulky. She did however try to nudge one last wedge of blackberry pie under his nose.

"It's raining down south, according to the weather report."

"He *likes* rain."

"Rains here all the time."

Lee stood. The night was clear and good for driving, provided he could persuade his wife to come with him. Now, finally, she did come, doing it sadly, as if her little suitcase had the whole weight of the world in it. Lee tried to shake hands with the woman, who refused. But when he went outside and looked back, he saw that she had flown to the window and was standing, watching continuously with hollow eyes.

"Lee!"

"We must." He started the engine, the woman at the same instant bursting out after them. She was not speedy, of course, but she was very strong; he was afraid the car might not break free of her grasp. And now she was shaking her fist at them and calling out something that could not be heard above the noise of the car.

Soon they were half a mile away, behind them a few flickering dots of light in the place called *Avalon*.

Chapter Nine

HISTORICALLY, IT WAS OLD HERE; NOR DID IT SURPRISE HIM IN THE LEAST
WHEN HIS HEADLIGHTS DISCOVERED AN ENORMOUS URN OF ETRUSCAN
TYPE, NOW ONCE AGAIN EXPOSED AFTER SO MANY CENTURIES. Next, a
house came up, inside it a thin man smoking nervously as fate
closed in. And then finally, somewhat after eleven o'clock, he
passed a massy structure where in old times the Elamites—Lee
drank—used to store their takings after each separate raid.

Thirty minutes later, they hit the trunk road and then turned
south again. A few grey cars were running home eagerly,
impatient for the trough and for bed. By hap, he had selected a
car that was like himself—it was at its best in the hours
between eleven and four. He was taken by the dashboard too,
a mysterious array that offered a blue-green light, very grainy,
that permitted him to find the brandy when it was needed.
And now finally, thirty miles into highway number 402, he took
out his Wagner tape and threw it into the machine, a gesture
that was much like drawing a gun. Certainly the combination
was just as deadly—Wagner, music, Judy, stars. When he died,
let it be from excess of beauty infinitely prolonged.

He was doing well, the Volvo behaving sweetly, when, just after midnight, he came upon a sight that chilled him to the bone—
a new-style woman in heels, ear bobs, the authorized hairstyle,
and a thousand dollars worth of clothes. Apparently her car

had broken down; Lee slowed, putting on a look of concern. Clearly what was needed here was some upper-body strength; he had some, she had none. Still wearing his concerned expression, he gave her twenty seconds to explain herself, a most risible effort of trying to communicate through the glass, which he declined to let down. He drank. She who had started out with her snotty face and general hauteur, now she was calling him "sir." No, no, no, the under-filth could rape her for what he cared, yes and many other things as well. Lee went on.

The land of Virginia came up suddenly out of nowhere. Till now, he had thought of it as a considerable place, and yet this tongue, or "Chersonese," as he called it, was narrow indeed. To west was a lighthouse, its upper stories no doubt crammed with an enviable library, while to east the immense Atlantic was showing some real irascibility, owing to its too-long confinement in one place. Lee kept one eye upon it at all times, even as he sailed into New Church, and then Oak Hall, and finally Temperanceville itself, a dowdy town where the people were perhaps only *too* sober. Lee drank. On the Chesapeake, a light gleamed evilly from Little Fox Island, but only then to disappear ever and again between the swells. He tried the radio, picking up a soft gibberish in which he believed he could detect a desperate plea emanating precisely from a distant ship so brightly lit up that it seemed to be on fire. The land, too, it had a doomed look. One time—he was sure of it—a notorious love affair had taken place just here.

Toward one, Judy came awake, sat wonderingly for a while, and then slumped off to sleep again. Suddenly the road lifted and then dove, plunging them far beneath the ocean. Lee was shocked—the Greeks would *never* have believed in the possibility of this—to be traveling faster than a horse could carry, and to do it under the sea. Nor would they have found credible a great giant truck like the one coming on to meet him, a monster with manifold eyes and blowing out steam. Looking closer, Lee caught a fleeting glimpse of a boy on a bicycle who, apparently, had been seized up in the truck's wake and was moving on toward New York far faster than ever he had intended.

They emerged upon the periphery of Norfolk itself, a pastel town, pretty from a distance but in fact an historical embarrassment when viewed up close. He moved slowly through the rich district, where even the homes seemed to be holding their noses at him. And although he kept his eye out for the rich people, he saw but one only, a nightmare face in a sports car. The car was a miracle of science and engineering, the driver himself pure rubbish, a pattern that seemed to hold for the century at large. Nothing now could rescue this population except a spate of huge suffering, perhaps by way of the "roasting machine" that he had been developing in his imagination.

He required a full hour before he could find the way out of town and get back to the highway. He had only just begun to acclimate himself to Virginia when, suddenly, to his shock, he found that he was now officially in North Carolina! This then was the *certifiable* South; he would have recognized it anywhere. Indeed, the very first house had a pot of flowers on the porch. He wanted to squeal, to get him down and kiss the earth, to run up onto the porch of that first house and wake the people, and show that he had come back; instead, he drank. Mayhap these past thirty years had not touched the South (the new generation holding out stubbornly in a latter-day Integrity Age), or mayhap they had; in any case, the night was mild.

He sliced into a small town with the courthouse on one side and a dark green woods on the other. The very last thing he wanted was to be caught in this part of the world while adorned with a New York plate; accordingly, he pulled in next to an expensive-looking car of German manufacture—it didn't seem to belong in North Carolina in the first place—and then, working quickly and effectively, exchanged tags with the thing. And even then he was still not satisfied, not until he had opened his pants and had urinated, doing it gratuitously and with high pleasure, direct into the other's high-priced tank.

He traveled on, into a strange section called "Burnt Hills." Here the clouds had cracks in them (the moon pouring through), and homes were made of pies and candy. One, even, had a grandmother on the porch who, amazingly, had chosen this time for churning out her weekly butter. Lee slowed and then began threading through a drove of hens migrating across the road. Fog was rolling in from the Perquimans. Ahead, a swineherd in straw hat had stopped and was very courteously pointing out the route with his staff. Now suddenly a tavern came up, a lantern glowing greenly over a sign swinging in the wind. So quickly had the fog gathered, Lee pulled off into the first road that was wide enough to admit him.

He had been looking forward to hearing his new *Tristan*, fog music indeed, and possibly also of opening a new bottle of brandy; instead, he found himself in an orchard loaded down with peaches. He rolled forward a few inches, actually plucking one of the things from his cockpit. At once, fog filled the cabin, hiding his wife and book collection both. She was small and possibly getting smaller, wherefore he lifted her more easily even than of two days ago. The sun, three hours too early, was making one of the brief reconnoiters of the sort to which he had become accustomed; he knew it would not stay. As to Judy, she slept soundly in his arms and would be of no use to him until the day had dawned truly. He carried her back therefore and set her up in the car. Somewhere a bell was tolling the hour. His strange career: four weeks ago he was perishing in an office building, and now he was tiptoeing through fog and fallen fruit in someone's well-tended orchard.

He listened to forty-five minutes of the music, until the protagonist was discovered lying out-of-doors with the gorgeous Isolde at his side. Lee groaned. Beauty on top of music on top of fog and Judy; this *was* the certifiable South. He might have waited out the entire opera in this place, had not then a light come on in the little farmhouse—and he could almost touch it—that had been cut off by the fog. Hurriedly he reaped another dozen peaches and then began to roll back toward the highway, refusing to start the motor until he was out of shotgun range. It was the certifiable South, and he knew what a shotgun could do.

The South was devastated still, he could have identified it anywhere. Here and there he spied a few forlorn figures standing out beside the highway without any apparent reason and simulating indifference whenever he approached too near. He hated for Judy to miss all this—a man leading a cow that was itself wearing a hat. He tried the radio, getting nought but preachers issuing pleas and following them up with threats. He came into the town called "Bethel," the most placid of places, but so full of churches that the rest of the economy had fallen into ruins. And then, too, the roadside signs were inscribed so glitteringly, it was as if the whole country were dressed in leftover jewels.

Old Sparta came up, a town without walls, now horribly reduced from what it must once have been. He broke through it and out the other side even at the same moment as the orange sun stood up suddenly and began sending its darts and arrows into all places. It was for this and nothing else that Judy had been waiting; looking at her, he saw a new wide-awake person, calm, tidy, and mild.

"Shall I drive now?"

He gave over to her. The sun had finished with its half-minute of absolute beauty and had turned into a routine thing of great annoyance. His wife did have a steady way with the car, the speed never varying and never, never breaking the law. Seen from behind, she was short, and had a bell-shaped head. Someday, they would be driving together through Paradise. Lee came forward and, without the woman being aware of it, sniffed tenderly in her divine hair. All the bright countryside hereabouts was cheerful, too cheerful, and naïve, too naïve to be anything other than a colored painting by a child. He saw a calf posing prettily—such had always been Lee's experience in North Carolina. And that, of course, was when the car broke down.

Chapter Ten

SMOKE WAS COMING OUT OF THE TAIL; NEVERTHELESS, HE WAS QUITE CHEERFUL. Propitiously, they were at the top of a hill and able to glide pleasantly for another quarter-mile in beautiful surroundings before having to be overly concerned. They passed a broad green field with yellow pigs in it. According to his philosophy, there must surely be a village down below. And then, too, he was listening to Rachmaninoff.

One could do far worse than be stranded in North Carolina. He stepped out, cheerful still, and addressed the four old men sitting shoulder to shoulder in front of the dry goods store. He knew these types, and knew how already they were rummaging through their inventory of sarcasms, the kind that might be described as "dry goods" too.

"Howdy!" said Lee (doffing his cap).

Two nodded, two did not.

"Warm, today."

"Little bit, yes sir."

"I believe it's warmer even than yesterday."

One nodded.

"Well! I'm not saying it's *too* warm, no, no, not at all. No, I simply feel that…"

"This great interest of yours in the weather, is it recent? Or long-standing?"

Lee was nonplussed. He hummed and looked off seriously into the distance where two blue mountains had come together in gorgeous conjunction not often to be seen. Then:

"So how'd your football team do this year?"

"Aw, Jesus Christ, 'football.' Look man, this here's the *new* South. You don't have to talk about football."

Three nodded, one was looking off into the mountains. That was when Lee noticed that of the group, only one was actually chewing tobacco.

"Seems like I'm having trouble with my car, and so I…"

"Wal! I wouldn't worry too terrible much if it just *seems* that way."

"No, actually I *am* having trouble. And so I…"

"Hey! That ain't Rachmaninoff I hear?"

Lee admitted that it was. He realized now that it was not at all the mountains, but rather his own pretty wife that they were so absorbedly watching. As for the requisite southern hound, theirs was lying face down in the dusk, grieving over its recently shortened tail.

"And so, in short, do you know of any mechanic in the county, the sort that could cope with a Volvo? As it were?"

A long silence. He could see that all four were searching in growing desperation for something dry and witty to say. Finally, the oldest and most parched of them:

"Why, you ain't got no *oil* in it! That's my opinion. Course now, I could be wrong, seeing how 'old and parched' you think I am."

"Oil." (Here, Lee had to smile.) "No, no, this is a *gasoline*–driven machine."

"Wal! Them Swedes!"

Lee hummed, but then had finally to come and interpose himself between the most inquisitive of them and his own pretty wife. That was when a fifth man, the driest of the lot, stepped suddenly from behind the corner post. He spoke. He would not, however, look a stranger in the eye.

"There's but one man in this county can fix a car like that." Again, he disappeared behind the column.

"Hold!" said Lee. "Which person? Where?"

"Fellow over to Durant's Neck."

"Neck! I can hardly hear you, there where you are."

"But I wouldn't recommend you consult with him, not on Wednesdays."

"It's Thursday."

"Wal!"

"Better take a present," said the third man. "That's my advice."

"Present?"

"Books, flowers. Strange perfumes."

Lee looked at them. For one brief moment he almost wished himself back in New York again.

"This 'fellow,' what would his name be, I wonder?"

"Mort," said the second man. "Leastways, that's what he calls himself on Wednesdays."

They laughed.

"You laugh," said Lee, "but I don't know why. Very well, tell me this: the way to Durant's Neck."

They had, in truth, a very long way to go. He set out in a glum mood that however began to ameliorate as soon as they came up over the first hill. The woman, she *never* regretted time spent in the field; he saw her first here and then there, at one point even taking out the little specimen box that she carried with her always. Here too the weeds were so extensive, so much like wheat itself, the view had that sea-like quality alluded to in Grecian literature. Lee slowed; he had no method for forestalling these aesthetic experiences, which so often came upon him at the most untoward of times. And now he began to wish it were a thirty-mile walk and not just three, and wished too that the sun might stay forever at just this tint and degree of pleasant warmth. Nor was there any sort of insect or bloom or seed pod or spider work but that

Judy must run and look at it, her mouth very often falling
open in pure delight. No doubt about it, she had a vocation
for the out-of-doors, for weeds and grasses and yes—Lee
stopped to watch her—for the faint distant shimmering bay
called *Albemarle*. And if he hated cities, primarily it was because
they infringed upon his desire that he and Judy should be
alone upon the world. There were no cities *here*; indeed, he
doubted whether any European had ever yet set foot just
where he was traveling. True, he could not wholly block out
the execrable "Elizabeth City," of which he had already had
too much on the downward voyage. Instead (and now Judy
was at his side), he focused upon the "wheat" (i.e., field
grasses interspersed with numerous blue flowers) that
seemed to run all the way down to the booming Atlantic
itself. As to the man "Mort," the blackguard had selected an
almost perfect locale for carrying out his Volvo repairs. Lee
had not seen loveliness like this since... Again, he stopped
and then retreated four paces in order to reacquire a certain
perspective that was peculiarly beautiful, the best of the
whole day.

"O!" said Judy. "The sky!"

"Yes."

"The clouds!"

"I'm not unaware of them."

In fact, he was looking at the woman. Always she had
been his own pretty wife, whereas now, here, deep in *Daphne
cneorum* and sneeze worts, she was girlish again and sparkling,
like unto the almost-forgotten Andromache, most honorable
of all wives. He didn't know whether he wanted more to
weep (recognizing that she too was on death's agenda, and
someday must also die) or to jump on her.

"And so many flowers!"

"Indeed. Now take off all your clothes and..."

"Please, Lee."

"...all your clothes and walk here—never mind how
deep it is!—just here where the 'wheat' is bending."

And she did so, albeit a little sadly at first. Lee followed at a distance, watching darkly till she grew comfortable with it at last, like Greek girls used to do. In paradise, she would go naked always.

"Hold! Very well, and now walk *toward me*."

And she did. He had seen all this countless times, but never like this, never with swift clouds. She was smiling, Lee trembling, the aesthetic experience continuing. All might still have been well, but for the sound of distant thunder.

This was no "three mile walk"; on the contrary, it seemed to Lee that he might after all get that thirty that he had so recklessly wished for when first starting out. Moreover, many times he lost sight of the sea altogether, but only then to find it again, further each time. "Wine," the Achaeans had called it, whereas to his mind he thought of it as naphtha, or "juice," or… No, no, the Achaeans had it—deep scarlet wine.

It was well into the afternoon before they entered Durant's Neck, an extinct place, as he imagined at first. Quickly they passed between the two fortified churches, the ramshackled *Nazarene Jubilee* on the one side, and the *New Voice in the Wilderness* on the other. Here in this place, it would always be three in the afternoon. One single inhabitant they saw, a woman in a kerchief who wanted obviously to get out of sight as quickly as she could. On the beach itself, he saw pieces of fishing equipment, a child's toys, and two fine-looking horses (their manes braided in bright red ribbons) playing joyously in and out of the surf.

They moved on, tiptoeing past a row of picturesque cottages with painted shutters and high-steeped roofs. Lee caught an elderly woman peeping out at them from an upstairs window, whereupon he turned and bowed sweepingly to her. Judy, meanwhile, had found a half-hidden garden in front of one of the houses, and had gotten down on one knee to look into it more closely.

"Why…! My God, this is nothing in the world but *henbane growth!* See those leaves?"

"Henbane!"

"Why, yes."

"And *those*, are they…?"

"No, no." Then: "Oh my word!"

Lee jumped.

"Foxglove too!"

"*Yellow* foxglove?"

"I thought so—digitalis. We ought to leave right now."

Lee trembled. There was a man (he *looked* like a man) standing just inside the door. Lee took off his cap.

"Howdy."

No response. Judy had gotten to her feet and was looking behind, as if prepared to race the whole thirty miles back to the car.

"Warm today," said Lee, smiling cordially. "Well! Not so *inordinately* warm, no. No, actually I *like* it this way, 'wine dark seas,' etc., etc." (He realized he was running on.) "My Volvo is broken."

"Volvo?"

"Just so. And I am led to believe there may be an individual in this town who…"

"I am that individual."

"Thought so." (They looked at each other closely. Lee was also able to peer somewhat into the cottage itself, where, it seemed to him, it was full of a number of things.)

"This Volvo, we're not talking about that old thing—no, no, don't look in *there*! Look at *me*, when you talk—of Tony's, are we?"

Lee was confused. He was not to look into the cottage, and yet he was absolutely certain of having seen a telescope, or some other instrument of similar profile. "Possibly," he said finally. "New York does after all have a great many 'Tonys.'"

"New York?" The man began to close the door. Lee managed just in time to cry out:

"But we're going south!"

The door came open. "Volvo?"

"Right."

"And are you giving it all the oil it wants?"

Lee could not but smile. "No, no, this is a *gasoline*-powered engine of which we speak."

"They too demand oil."

"The devil you say!"

"Why certainly. And you—do *you* thrive on one fluid alone?"

"No," said Judy. "He doesn't."

"Well I'll be jiggered. Oil!"

"And so I'll say goodbye now, while wishing you fair weather on your long walk."

"Wait!" said Lee. "I brought some peaches for you."

Again the door came open, though only narrowly. Lee had to pass the things in to him, bruised as they were from the thirty-mile jaunt.

"Thank you indeed; very, very thoughtful. And now I'll bid you a pleasant…"

"Wait! I couldn't help but notice how you have a great many books in there." (He pointed to them.) "Shelves and shelves."

"Yes?"

"But have you *read* them all—*that's* what I ask."

They looked at each other. Never had Lee seen so unhealthy a type, it being a marvel that the man could stand up without help.

"The better part of them."

"You mean to say you've read *most* of them? Or those that are better?"

"The better part of the most of them. Well, goodbye now."

"Wait! And did I see a *telescope* in there?"

The man sighed deeply, looked imploringly to heaven, and then sighed again. "Come in, come in, come in, Sweet Jesus! You too, Judy; I can see there's no way around it."

"Much obliged," said Lee. "Coffee, too, if you would." (He had expected a routine collection of books, trash novels and the like; instead, seeing what he saw, he leaped back. Always heretofore he had thought his own collection to be the most pernicious anywhere.

"Caedmon too? Nothing surprises me anymore. But where do you keep your Greeks?"

The man sat staring at him fixedly. He had not yet made the first effort to prepare coffee.

"I'm not partial to your 'Grecians,' if I may be so allowed."

Lee could feel his gorge rising. He spent a minute trying to control it. The pistol had been left behind with the car. Judy, meanwhile, had raised her hand and was waiting to be recognized.

"Yes?"

"Your garden…"

"So?"

"Bad things. I know what I saw."

Now was it the man's turn to blush and seem to grow confused.

"May I bring the coffee now?"

"Coffee? But who knows what you might put in it!" Lee laughed, uproariously so, stopping only when he saw that he was laughing alone. For the second time, he wished he had stayed behind in New York. Outside, the podgy sun had now come down to five o'clock level, where the birds were picking at it.

"You must have been driving very crookedly," the man said, "to have come to these parts."

"He won't drive in the daytime."

"One of those! What, can't endure to look at the late century in full light? Yes, yes, I see it all: fleeing New York, stolen car, peaches." (He sat thoughtfully, plucking at his chin.) "Tell me, and is your car also full of stolen books?"

"You have more books than I."

"I'm older."

"No, just more unhealthy."

"Blunt talk, coming from *you*. My unhealth, as it happens, has a very good cause."

"Drugs."

"No, no, no."

"Too much ascetic practice."

"No, no."

"Genetics."

"No. Father was a wholesome man."

"Grandfather."

"*That* one was wholesomer yet."

Lee could feel his gorge rising again. Nothing could be more exasperating than to be face to face with an intellectual whose arrogance was perhaps as advanced as Lee's own. "Your unhealth, it's owing to spiritual accomplishment—is *that* what you wish to claim?"

"You must admit, it *is* a good site for it."

"The sea on one side…"

"Yes."

"…mountains on the other."

"Yes. And poor dumb villagers, a fish-eating people, each of them more ignorant than the other; perhaps you observed them on your downward voyage?"

"And these 'poor dumb' ones, I suppose they have no notion of what you're carrying on in this cottage?"

"None."

"The 'sciences' you practice here?"

"No notion at all. Nor do you, for that matter. Well, goodbye now."

Lee looked at him, a noble profile silhouetted against a book array, a microscope, two computers. Also some hundred sealed beakers with, each of them, a marine specimen of some sort floating in dark serum. Lee asked:

"Which city did you escape from?"

"You ask. I speak the solemn truth when I say that although I remember the building very well…"

"You don't recall the town."

"Sorry."

They laughed merrily. The man, who was having trouble in sitting up straight, now opened one eye slightly, allowing the grey pupil to be seen. A minute passed. Outside, the sun-wheel had dipped to within inches of the bay, casting a path of gold, as it were, on which it seemed that one might actually be able to set foot, and actually walk.

"The sun…"

"Yes. 'Shamash,' we used to call him. As to that 'path of gold,' it's much the same as in dying."

Lee looked at him. Judy, too, she was watching in interest, alarm, concern.

"Oh yes, many times I've died. And you needn't screw up your face like that either—I won't have it."

"Let me understand this—you've died *many times?*"

"Wednesdays, usually. Oh well, sometimes I indulge on a Saturday as well, or even Sundays."

"Henbane!"

"No, actually one develops an immunity to that rather quickly. No, I use a more reliable stuff now."

Lee stood, and then sat. The man went on:

"Antidote—*that's* the dubious part. Fortunately, there's a good woman in the village who's willing to help."

"But… But… Heavens above…!"

"Heavens, yes; oh, I've seen it all."

"You're not going to tell us…"

"Religion? I'm talking *physics*, man. I'm talking that 'wormhole' that leads on to…"

"Wisdom?"

"Pshaw! You ought to know better than that."

"Beauty?"

The man glanced up with new interest.

"Been there, have you?"

"No, no. Ha! No, no. But I *would* like to hear about it."

"Me too."

"Especially the 'wormhole.'"

130 The man sighed. He had poured a drink for himself (offering none to his guests), a cloudy liqueur with much sediment and berries floating in it. Outside, the sun had finally touched down some minutes ago, but then had arisen again very slightly, there to linger. They waited. A minute passed. *Now* came the story:

"We fell, and falling…"

"'We?'"

"Yes, certainly; I don't go *alone*, for Christ's sake." (He nodded to a small dog that Lee had not until this moment observed. It was a withered creature, watery eyed, apparently in as much ill health as the man.)

"Ah! Continue please."

"No more interruptions?"

"I swear it."

"I swear too."

He sighed. On the beach, a crowd of pelicans had formed a circle wherein two of their number were dueling with beak and claw. Others of them, disdaining to watch, were standing on top of the pilings. For a moment, Lee thought his host had fallen off to sleep; instead, at the last moment, he roused himself as if by an act of will, and then proceeded to tell the story rather hurriedly, employing phrases and a tone of voice that indicated that it had been told before.

Chapter Eleven

"**W**E FELL, AND FALLING, THOUGHT THAT LIFE INDEED WAS DONE. Falling and drowning, drowning and spinning, head over heels tumbling and yet, oddly, no fear whatsoever. No fear! Even though I had always been one of the most fearing of persons."

"But…"

"I'm coming to that."

They looked at each other steadily, till Lee weakened at the sight of his grey dead eyes.

"Will you allow me to come to it in my own fashion? I need to know."

"Proceed, proceed."

"We fell, and falling, thought the night indeed had come. Falling and spinning, turning and tumbling, head over heels, and the rest of it. Imagine therefore our dismay, the horror of it: to gaze down in detachment—and I use that word in both senses—to gaze down, I say, upon one's *own corpse and husk!* Unspeakable. To tell the truth, I had never really seen myself from that particular angle."

"Never knew he had a bald spot," said Lee, whispering to his wife.

"Hideous. Far more presentable was the cadaver of my courageous dog." (He summoned the thing now and sat, his eyes mere slits, while he petted and measured the animal's paper-thin ears between his thumb and finger.) "Horrible, horrible."

"Proceed."

"We drifted, and drifting, thought the ceiling all too low."

"Much too low."

"And expired again."

"Again!"

"Cave or cavern, tube, tunnel or barrel, call it what you will if only you'll believe how thick the traffic was. Advertisers, realtors, consultants, all of them quite denuded of form and substance, a vision so unutterable… You're quite sure you want to hear this?"

Judy, pale, nodded hesitantly.

"Consultants. Nay, one I saw had actually done consultancy for a public relations firm! Yes, yes, you may well make a face like that, *their* faces showed the fear that is *real*." He coughed, drank, and then went on:

"No doubt you had imagined that some kindred soul, some person you had loved and admired, no doubt you had thought that such a one would fly to your aid at so critical a moment—is that what you thought?"

Lee shrugged, but then finally did admit it. "Yes."

"Your ancient Alabama grandmother perhaps? Mahler or Nietzsche or Wagner—somebody like that? Oh come on, man! Some Greek or another? Um? Let's have it."

Lee gave his answer, but in so small voice that none could hear it.

"You gave your answer, but in so small voice that none could hear it."

Lee gave it again, this time *too* loudly. "Poe, I'll take Poe."

"You sure about that?"

"Could I have two?"

"No you can't have two! Gad. And now I suppose you had imagined that there was some divisioning off of the good souls from the bad, a separation of the integrity people from the careerists and whatnot, hm? A special fate for the Philistines— is that what you thought? Hm? Voters, sports fans?"

"I have always hoped so."

"Rejoice then."

"You mean to say…?"

"Just so."

Lee reeled, the joy leaping up in him in streaks of pure delirium. "Oh! *Oh!*"

"And as to that 'roasting machine' of yours—you couldn't really have believed that you dreamt it up out of nothing? Or did you? Why, you're no more capable of building such a thing than that you could…"

"Heal a car?"

They both laughed merrily. Lee liked him better now. Judy, however, who took no pleasure in punishments, she had gone outside and was stroking the dog. Lee waited while the man finished his drink and poured another, and then proceeded to drain off most of it as well.

"But how about that 'life's review' that is said to be enjoined upon the recently dead?"

"'Enjoined,'" the man said slowly, repeating it as if in a dream. "'Life's review.' Yes, there *is* such an enjoinment. I myself, however, I was not so enjoined until my third or, it may have been, my fourth visit."

"And you could see your whole life? As if from a mountaintop? The entire extent of it compressed into five seconds—as they say—including the worst and the best? With your own personal favorite historical figure standing at your side?"

He laughed heartily. "But I can see why they might describe it that way, that which cannot be described. No, no; life, like matter too, is mostly empty space. No, what I *did* see was a certain summer morning when I was perhaps some five or six years of age—that I *did* see."

"Go on."

"That's all—summer morning. Did I say that it was a particularly lovely one? And, of course, my late beloved wife—I was allowed to see recent pictures of her."

"But why not the wife itself! Why not to enfold her within your very arms!"

"No, no, no." (He laughed cheerfully.) "Not allowed, that. For, you see, I never *really* died."

"Never really died," said Lee, whispering it to Judy, who had come back and was sitting quietly.

"No. The truly dead mayn't come back, not at all. No, I'm just a habitual visitor, so to speak, nibbling about the edges."

"But…"

"Why elect to come back? Well! So that I could tell it to thee! After all, I am he who years ago foresaw that you'd be arriving in a car full of peaches, drawing nigher and nigher to this place while driving before you your lovely undressed wife."

The house was in full dark now, save only for the dim light from the two weak bulbs that illuminated the aquarium. In lieu of bookends, the man had used bottled specimens, one of them now twitching violently in a useless effort to break free. The village itself—perhaps the man had poisoned the lot of them; from where he sat, Lee could see two hollow homes with not even so much as furniture inside. True, one small ship was bobbing on the tide, a lilac-colored lantern bobbing with it. Lee waited for, and heard, the inevitable foghorn with its woeful call.

"Well," said Lee, getting up from his place. "I suppose we must…"

"Yes, yes, I'd be glad for it if you left now. But first, I must ask that you not try to make off with that book—I haven't read it yet, nor was it authored by any Greek that you or I ever heard of."

Lee blushed deeply, handing it over with an abashed air. Even so, he would still have been glad to remain a few days, and to acquire as much as possible of the man's knowledge, which was so much more exquisite by far than any that he had taken from books.

"Or, perhaps we should stay a few days and…"

In fact, the door had been shut in his face. They stood for a moment looking at it (the door) even as the man himself ran around to the window and peeped out at them through the blinds, his face showing an unfriendly expression. They moved off, Lee reluctantly, Judy gladly. And when they had gone a distance and turned to look back, it was only another steep-gabled roof they could see, together with a living rooster on it simulating a weather vane. They must tread quietly now, lest the village grow aware of their presence. Not that either of them was in a mood for talking! Quite the contrary. They had been talking all day, traveling too, and listening as well.

Soon the town was far behind and with nothing to show for it except two dim lights so feeble and so far away… He now doubted whether any such place had ever actually existed. All this had him deep in thought when suddenly, that moment, a dolphin or leviathan, or some equal creature, made a great breach on the leeward side where they had imagined the sea would be asleep by now.

"Gosh!"

They waited. Though he hadn't noticed it before, there was definitely another "neck" of land on the eastern horizon, pine-clad, as it looked to him, and so low in the ocean that it too might also have been a giant dolphin taking its leisure at the surface. Seldom was Lee vouchsafed *two* aesthetic experiences in one day, and *never* with a fascinating thousand-death man sandwiched in between. There was a fine wind off the gulf (a salt-bearing smell in it) and a good number of gulls overhead consorting—so it appeared—with a like number of bats. Never had he thought to see these two species having to do with each other. He knew this, that plunged into thought as he was, yet was his shoe full of sand.

They came over the hill. On his left-hand side, he had a whole wide continent, meadowland, some of it, and the rest set aside for cities; while on his right, he could look out over, first, a pink estuary, secondly a "spit," and then finally the fantastic Atlantic stream itself, a continent in its own right with, he knew, more and larger rivers in it (some sluggish, some not) than anything on land. Could anything be more strange than this: to gloat at the top of his intellectuo-moral development while standing in a high place in dramatic surroundings and knowing that life was more than half-finished?

"We're old," he said, "old and dying" (the woman said nothing), "and the next time that leviathan (or whatever it was), the next time she breaches, we'll be gone."

The woman said nothing. He had his height on her and could look down upon the top of her bell-shaped head. The night was *his* time, never hers, wherefore she was having to struggle, her duck-like feet splayed out too far for trodding on sand.

"But soon enough we'll be on firmer land," he said, adding: "A very great many bright stars are out tonight!"

The woman said nothing. In fact, his mind was thinking about the moon, so shockingly decayed since last he had examined it. Somewhere, far away, two hounds were baying insults at it.

"And then, on firmer ground, we'll travel more efficaciously, much!"

The woman said nothing. She was tired. Looking down upon her, he fell in love again, as was his wont.

"I'm thinking of getting down on the ground with you."

Now she paid heed. "No Lee, please; please not here."

"Too late!"

"No! No!"

"Oh yes indeed! Before we die! Now take off all your clothes, dear—yes, that's right—and lay them straight."

And she did so, albeit somewhat reluctantly at first, knowing as she did that the thousand-death man was seeing all. How lovely she was! Or was it that after certain years, she had become the prototype of her own special gender? Especially he liked her lying full on top of him, the fillip of a sky of stars just over her shoulder.

"Ah! Leave me never, though you be dressed in what Time must brush away." Actually, he said:

"Such stars! And what a lot of inhabitants on them too."

"Tell me."

"Green giants I see, and scads of dwarfs."

"*Red* giants, you meant to say."

"As you will. Lo! I think I see…!"

"What!"

"Explosion! Big one too. Yes, a very big explosion of ten billion years ago it was, the evidence of it only just now coming down to thee, and to me."

She shivered. Warm was she, brown and small, the same warm, brown, small one that had catered to his youth and was catering still.

"You *are* my wife," he said, "gorgeous still, and we have spent these many years. And yet, someday you may wake to find the other gone away!"

"No, Lee, please." Actually, she said:

"But I'll not leave thee dear, not now nor never, though we both be dressed in what Time must brush away."

In actual truth, she said:

"What else [do you see]?"

"Faces, some smiling, and some in stars."

"Faces comprised of stars?"

"Just so. And some with beards."

"Beards! Imagine."

"And lines of printed wisdom unscrolling just now before my eyes."

"All that? May I look too?"

"Absolutely not! No, you're not to budge before I give the word." (For he was running his hand up and down her lovely back and had no will to stop it. He never felt they were truly together until they were together truly, which is to say gazing into one another's eyes at very close range. In fact, it was *there* he read his lines of wisdom, in eyes wiser than the stars.)

"O leave me never," he said, saying it this time in real voice.

"But I'll not leave thee dear, now nor never, not till Time hath…"

"Look! Shooting star!" Then: "Also, nearer at hand, an airplane flying at too low elevation and no chance of reaching harbor."

She shivered violently. Being what she was, she took no consolation in other people's impending crashes. Lee looked at her, thinking:

"And if she be good, and he be not, yet oh leave him never!"

It was near dawn when they stumbled into town and found the four dry ones (two of them fast asleep) still loitering on their bench.

"Wal!"

(Lee saw at once the number of peach pits that had been spat out onto the ground.)

"You find that 'Mort' fellow?"

"We found him."

"Now that's one feller you don't never want to visit on Wednesday." (They grinned.) "No, sir! He ain't much good at conversation *then*, sitting up in that big chair of his."

"Your car's real cool now," said man number four.

"And not as heavy," said number three, spitting out a pit. Behind them, the dry goods proprietor had come out in his apron and was chewing rapidly on a substance of some kind. For the life of him, Lee could not account for why they were still up and abroad this early, a full hour before the sun—not until he noticed a small but growing traffic across the road at the Mount Moriah Holiness Assembly, where, according to the placard, a day-long workshop was promised, covering new management techniques.

Chapter Twelve

THEY WERE FALLING RAPIDLY NOW—SUCH WAS THE SOMEWHAT TENUOUS CHARACTER OF SOUTH CAROLINA. Not that it lacked hills and farms and the rest of it; say rather that it had been unfairly condemned to remain forever in North Carolina's more noble shade. They might spy an orchard here, a lake there, and yet he could never forget that they were moving further and further from the Atlantic stream and nearer and nearer to his own native lands, which he dreaded more and more even as New York itself slipped finally out of sight forever, the last slim building yielding at last to the almighty divide called *Blue Ridge*, even though the ridge was grey. He had a headache; moreover, he had been given an inferior grade of gasoline, judging by the fits and starts and popping sounds emitted by the car.

It was past noon when they collided with the abysmal *Quitsna*, a miserable-looking location (he had just come off highway number 17 and was already in a surly mood), and coasted into a service station.

"Oil!" he bawled out. "More oil!" And yet, instead of the attendant that he had every right to expect, it was a huge dog that came out and jumped up and stood looking in at him with loathing and hatred. He had forgotten the character of these southern hounds and their indignation. This one, apparently, remembered the car and, possibly, remembered the former owner too. Lee decided to quit the place at once.

He had but one remaining opera and when *it* finished, the clouds suddenly parted. He could see the sun in the mirror; more importantly, it could see *him*. He drank. Fore and aft, he was passing the tragic southern land in review, some in corn, some in cattle, and some (but very little) in tobacco too. Someday he hoped to drive all over it in more detail, once these last remnants of farms had given up and gone in to join with the cities.

When he woke for the third time, he found that Judy was driving, and he himself was in the rear along with the books (uncomfortable), and clothes and blankets (better). It was not unpleasant. And if up north it might already be blustery, here it was a balmy day. Lee drank. He had counted some mellow days in his life, and some that were dappled; *this* day was dappled, mild, pied, limpid, mellow, and, yes, brindled to boot. Suddenly, he clapped hand over mouth to keep from laughing out loud. It was Judy. She was driving, driving well, but had a wild look to her, together with two wisps of hair flying out behind.

He woke in Alabama.

"No!" he said, "not possible. It's not possible to cross all the distance from Durant's Neck in just one day, not unless…"

The woman said nothing.

"…unless you were using the main roads!"

She said nothing. That it *was* Alabama, he could read it both in people's faces and in the blood-red clay. The flora, too, it had that admixture of passion flowers, of thorns, scuppernongs, and magnolias—he would have known it anywhere. Quickly he slipped to the other window, finding evidence of mule bones along the roadbed and, amid it all, a thirty-year-old crop of cotton never harvested. By no means was he so certain of this "New South," and whether it would measure up to his liking or not.

"Grist mills—where are they?" He *did* see his first Negress, a black nymph, nubile beyond belief and dripping with hormones. It gladdened his heart, until he recognized that she was behind the wheel of a Japanese car and dressed in a business suit. His gorge did rise; he liked his black people *poor*, poor and wretched, poor, wretched, and picturesque (for in him, the aesthetical had long ago overborne the ethical), yes, and liked his farm wives in bonnets and adorable little shoes of wood. And now, instead of pickup trucks with hard-looking drivers, in fact he was being offered an endless line of near-new cars with suits in them. He wanted to puke. "Agrarian Civilization" indeed! Lee saw no agrarians anywhere.

It was in the afternoon of the twenty-seventh day that they began to enter the outskirts of the small north-northeast Alabama town that Lee had been describing for thirty years, forcing his wife to listen. His excitement was too much to contain. His friends, his many friends, he must not look for them among the twelve-year-olds. The post office came up, formerly a monumental pile, as he remembered it, but now only a small town government building. It hurt him to see a video rental in the place where he used to buy his fishing tackle. Came next the dress shop. He could remember the farm wives (too shy to enter) and how they used to stand outside looking in hungrily while plucking at their chins over this or that simple yellow dress. And now the place had been taken over by a specialist in rubber and leather. The bakery came up, transmogrified beyond all recognition into a suntan salon. He wanted to weep. Two doors further was the movie house (now closed and sealed), where once he had sat hand in hand, shivering in the dark, with a certain well-known beauty of eleven years of age.

They parked, Judy waiting while he got out and strolled fifty yards in one direction (he had traveled over this stretch thousands of times), before turning and coming back.

"Does it seem like home?"

"Oh it does! A little bit."

"Do you see anyone you know?"

"That one?" (He had his eye on a tall man making toward them. He was of the right height certainly, but whether it was actually that fine ball player of 1953… Lee was not persuaded.) Unfortunately, the town was full of new-style people, late-twentieth-century types (mouths dangling open in late-twentieth-century stupor), most of whom had not even been born when Lee himself was already taking girls to movies.

"These people…"

"I know."

"And there! Why, that's where we used to get our ice cream!"

"I know, I know. Don't look at it."

"And now they're selling…"

"Software. Shall we go now?"

They drove for half an hour, his astonishment increasing. Finally, at the corner of Tenth and Quintard, he again left the car to follow after a somewhat bedraggled sort of person with a bag over his shoulder and with an even more bedraggled-looking dog shambling along behind him. Lee reckoned him at perhaps forty years of age, old enough to have remembered the late phases of Lee's own career in the town. However, the man moved so slowly… Lee put on a burst of speed, running past him and going on for another twenty yards before turning and coming back. He did want to give the fellow every chance in the world of recognizing him, and of doing it of his own volition. Indeed, he expected any second now to hear the man exclaim out loud—Lee grinned—and then to come forward with his hand extended; in fact, they passed without words.

"Please, Lee." (She had been following in the car, very worried looking.)

"Son-of-a-bitch! I'll *make* him recognize me, even if I have to… And after all the things I did in this town!"

Again he ran forward, passing the man and then turning and coming back. He saw no recognition in those eyes, none. Moreover, after the third effort, the dog began to growl. It was on the fourth try that Lee planted himself squarely in the man's path. That was when he perceived that one of his eyes had gone bad, all the color having apparently been siphoned out of it.

"Well then" (said Lee), "now I can partly understand why you didn't recognize me. Naw, it's alright."

"What?"

"Me. Remember?" Lee grinned. "1955?"

"He won't bite." Then: "Yeah, yeah; seems like I *do* remember, yeah."

"And '56?"

"Yeah! *You* were that one…"

Smiling modestly, Lee nodded and looked off afar.

"It was you!"

"Yep."

"Jesus O'Mally Shit! When did they let *you* out?"

"They didn't *let* me. I had to *crash* out, so to speak."

"Oh shit."

"And Lloyd, what's *he* doing these days? I think about him all the time."

"Lloyd."

"Not still going with Alice, I don't suppose. Or maybe he is! Ha! Is he?"

"Wouldn't be surprised. Well, I got to get going now."

"And Elaine!"

"Good ole Elaine. Well, reckon I'd better…"

"Jerry! People used to think *he'd* be the one to marry her. Did he?"

"Please, Lee."

"Yeah, yeah. I just moved here last year, you understand."

"And Charlie T.! Hey, I'm talking."

"Lee!"

He sat in the front seat, his attitude sullen. Of these houses passing slowly in review, there was not one of them that had not contained a boy or girl whom he had been in habit of visiting. This in fact was the *world* town, the true one, and all the others must forever remain as mere poor simulacra of greater or lesser veritude.

Two blocks further, they parked in front of the school, itself dark, abandoned, and falling apart. He was not prepared for the emptiness where recently so many large-eyed children, awed by the immensity of it all... And now they survived only as very short ghosts, clusters of them blundering about in memory wherever he looked.

He went upstairs, and then into a side chamber furnished with miniature toilets. The classroom itself was small, laughably so, and yet what a lot of education (*mid*-century education) had taken place just here. To his delight, the blackboard still had some little vestige of wisdom on it, factual data touching upon Monroe and 1812.

He went out and drove away. It was a clear day, much like those he remembered, save that now the youth of the West had all passed away. As he remembered it, people were excitable in those days, and full of every sort of unjustifiable optimism; now, every face he saw seemed imprinted with a sneer.

He drove past Quintard, past Noble Street, and then into the slum that had always been forbidden to him when he was young, a breeding ground for athletes and for the vivid girls who wore hose and lipstick before they were thirteen. It did him good to find that the neighborhood still did have girls in it. It did him bad, however, to see the expression on their faces. Gone the lipstick, gone the vividness; what he saw now was blank extinction. He wanted to cry. Nor had he needed to come home to see his thesis proved, namely that here too life had been falling off precipitously in his absence, and quality was down.

He pulled into a station and then, after clamoring for oil, went to use the room. Here, late-twentieth-century wits had written such things on the walls as could not have been imagined at mid-century. Outside, the attendant was dealing with the Volvo while at the same time gazing in at Judy in a way that Lee did not like. There was something about this person, something in the shape of the head. Lee went to him, moving cautiously, till he could see the face as well.

"Dwayne? Good Lord! I *thought* I recognized something in that head. This is *me!* Me!"

"I seen you."

"Good Lord! Dwayne!"

"Right. Want me to check under that hood?"

"Good Lord! Dwayne. Why, I haven't seen you since…"

The man looked at him coolly. He was corrupt, also unhealthy looking. And if he had been a leading figure in '53, now his face had turned a bright brilliant red with boils on it.

"Good Lord! Naw, it's alright; I drink too much too. Whew!" Then: "But you're not going to tell me you *like* this period in history?" Then: "Divorced, are you?" Then: "Hey! I always wondered: what ever happened to Sam and Joyce?"

"I don't keep track of stuff like that."

"And Alice! What ever happened to Alice?"

"Alice Belinsky? Hell, I don't know. Want me to look under that hood? Or not?"

A car had pulled in and was blowing impatiently. Lee tried to keep the man's attention.

"And Billy! What happened to Billy?"

"Billy? Shit, he died so long ago… Shit, I almost forgot about him."

"Died!"

"Got hisself kilt." He grinned.

"No!"

"Well, I gotta go. Look, y'all come back sometime."

"What about Jo!"

He was gone; Lee watched him lift someone else's hood and, chewing, look under it.

Now the countryside began to decline very rapidly. Never had he seen so much rubbish, so many bottles and cans and abandoned trucks, all of it pushed off onto the shoulder of the road, providing apartments for the crickets. Lee let down the window to listen to their song.

They crossed the Coosa, full of islands. This evening, it was a blue sheet in which a certain number of fishermen had petrified up to the tops of their wading boots. Nor was the forest in good condition. He saw where the trees had been snapped off alongside an unfinished highway with heavy equipment left out to rust. Next, a swampy area, and a black man pilgrimaging across a field toward no destination that Lee could perceive. A fire had broken out in the hills, one of the most evil that Lee had ever witnessed; he thought he could see men dressed in cow skulls dancing about the flames. Nothing surprised him anymore, not the fire and not the coyote (or whatever it was) that ran out in front of him that moment and turned to reveal a humanoid face.

He scrambled for his Wagner tapes, not wishing to waste such a night as this. He did so admire the dark; darkness it was, and nothing else, that kept the majority of humankind locked up in their homes where they rightly belonged, and where he wanted them always. Lee drank. Behind him, a dangerous-looking car had bolted out suddenly from one of the side roads and was following so closely, so quietly and so undeviatingly, that Lee began to feel concerned. There was also another car following the one that was following him. People whom he had wronged at one time? Waiting all these years? He slowed and then, having verified that they refused to pass, he began to grow alarmed in real truth.

He drank and increased the music and then, with great foreboding, turned to find that the man was driving side by side with him now, inch for inch. Seldom had Lee observed so much hatred in a single human face; he was glad that Judy (sleeping) couldn't see it. It took him longer than he liked to hunt down the revolver and then, working with one hand alone, to load it with two fat cartridges. The driver was speaking furiously (though Lee couldn't hear it), his face contorted with all the rage of thirty-six years. Thus they ended up staring at each other, right up until the moment Lee brought the pistol into view and allowed the man to look at it. *Now* he dropped off, to be immediately swallowed by traffic, and so quickly that Lee no longer knew which car it was.

The music was *so* good, and the night so big, he felt as though he were pushing deeper and deeper into the more unexplored regions of sweet death itself. Here, now, finally, at last, all things were falling into place. He had his divine wife sleeping at his side, his home state, a car too (its bay full of books), brandy he had, gun, and some of the best versions of some of the most exquisite music ever writ. For to him, music also was a "tool," one that allowed him to leverage himself, if only briefly, into the domain of metaphysics. A car came up to meet him and then, seeing that Lee was grinning and waving his arm about to the music, put its lights on bright.

Twenty miles still to go before Birmingham, and yet already he could see certain indications in the sky—airplanes, gas flares, etc. A motorcycle came up and passed him, a noisy thing constructed out of junk and carrying two wild-looking girls in goggles and shorts. The city itself seemed to be in some chaos; resorting to the radio, he was able to pick out nothing but static and popping sounds, until suddenly an urgent voice, direct from Washington, came on to announce that in the latest period, housing starts were up. Comestibles, however, were down; he could hear groaning from the new-started houses. Just then, three searchlights sprang up from points along the perimeter and began raking frantically across what was truly a threatening-looking sky. He sped past a stadium that was so brightly lit, with so many people crowded into the stands, that he could only assume it must be another beer-flag-and-Jesus ceremony—he knew them well!—with the usual public disembowelments.

He used another hour in getting *through* town, and *out* of it, and once more into the authentic countryside. These were undulating lands here; he could read into it that "universal empire" against which Toynbee had warned. Finally, just after midnight (Judy asleep), he pulled off, leaving highway number 20 forever and entering a narrow road cut into the clay hills. There was a service station, closed for the night, but with a soft-drink machine glowing oddly in the interior. A mile further, he came upon a deer feeding in the roadside garbage, and then next, a bare ruined barn with curled tin roof. The landscape was irreparable, blighted for all eternity, the consequence of a wickedness so great that it didn't matter how much time might pass. Suddenly they ran over a clattering bridge that spanned the river, a vile vein of blood sparkling redly in the moon. He knew they had entered the county as soon as he heard the dour hymnology of the frogs, thousands of them lined up elbow to elbow along the banks of the Cahawba—this, at least, had *not* changed. Lee now reached for his bottle and finished it, and then, to prove that he was a southerner too, tossed it out cynically to lie with the other clutter. There was virtually no traffic, saving only one debilitated truck with a conservative bumper sticker and a carbine mounted in the rear.

He went on, swinging off at last onto a dirt road that climbed into the hills. That he was being watched by dead people, and being discussed, that his wife (never before seen in these parts), that she especially was being discussed… He passed a wooden church, now fallen into sadness. To be sure, the *kudzu* was thriving; he spotted a long green tendril of it worming across the road. Somewhere too a dog was yapping desultorily, with no real conviction. A home came up, an old-fashioned thing, two stories high, with a swing on the porch and pieces of farm machinery in the yard. It was here that Lee caught the dog in his beams, a cowardly figure striving to hide behind the tractor.

Even a dog counted for something in a region like this one, with a population so thin and houses so far apart. He passed a ruin, formerly a store where the farmers used to gather. Next came a teetering chimney standing quite alone in the field, the home itself having long ago been burnt by invading Picts. A shed had burst asunder, spilling out a quantity of rotting cotton that looked like brains. The road was poor; he was obtruding into a place where the people wished only to be left alone and allowed to suffer in peace. That moment, the crickets left off singing, even at the same instant that a lantern came on in the woods.

He turned in at the lane that he remembered so well. Now the way was faded, and he had to take care not to stray off into the field. He did dread what might lie at journey's end, and the chance that they had come for nothing, with only a void where once there had been a house. (In truth, he still half hoped to find the place lit up brightly, and all his people gathered on the porch in welcome.) Instead, he saw a wretched little building, far, far smaller than he remembered, and covered in barnacles.

He parked. And yet, this once had been the center of the world, before he had set out upon his tremendous achievements. And now he was glad that none could see him slinking back, a failed scholar in a stolen car, in worse state than when he had left.

He got out and stood face to face with it, a coruscated structure that had turned black over the ages and glistened now among the flowers. Objects lay in the yard (the yard itself having gone back to weed), including an icebox lying on its side.

He went around to the back and then stepped the few paces to the edge of the gulch where in earlier times he used to hear faint distant voices welling out of the depths. In those days, he

150

had been the only one to realize it, that unauthorized Negroes were living in the valley on land that was not their own. Just then, a tissue of smoke floated up in front of him and snagged on the branches. He heard a radio (very, very weak and very, very far away), and then next, a child calling out briefly at three o'clock in the morning and from two miles down in the valley.

He came back, lifted his wife as gently as he could, propped her against an oak, and then started for the house. The door, such as it was, was sealed; finally he drew back and smashed it in with his foot.

He was shocked by the volume of bad air that rushed to effectuate its escape, and shocked too by the uncanny smell. A bird flew out past him in great panic. Nor was he willing to step inside without first going back for the flashlight and pistol.

The place was in an awful state. He had to clamber over a hill of fallen plaster, wet and earthen in color. The great portrait of his grandfather was still in place, but so hurt by

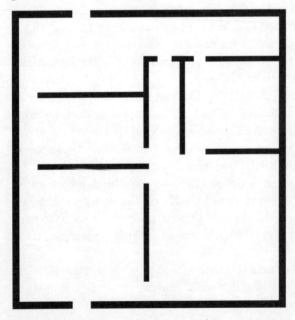

damp that the man seemed to be looking out through bad dreams. The cabinet, his grandmother's pride, was lying on its face—this done deliberately—and all its contents reduced to a rubble in which someone had been trodding back and forth happily every day. The center room, the same in which he used to fall off to sleep by staring at the fire and embers, had now a mattress on the floor together with two soiled blankets, food, and a quantity of pornographic magazines. The truth fell in upon him—that someone had taken up occupancy and perhaps was living here still.

He peeped into the bathroom, finding it hopeless, the toilet lacking, the bathtub having been used for cleaning fish. And yet, the kitchen seemed hardly to have been affected. The flour bin was intact, indeed had some little bit of powder in it still. The stove was in its place; he could imagine what Judy would think of *this*—a great black massive business that had proved too troublesome to topple over, or to toss out into the yard. Suddenly he spun about to find Judy herself standing in the doorway.

"I woke," she said, "but you were not there!"

"Hopeless, here. Look at it."

"What do you mean?"

"Hopeless. We'll just have to keep going. Florida, I suppose."

"What do you mean, 'hopeless?'"

"Look at it."

"We could fix it."

"Oh good."

"Well what else are we going to do! Florida, ha! We don't have any acres in Florida, not one!" (She was short but stubborn and, in her middle years, possibly getting *more* stubborn. Lee led her out quickly to the edge of the cliff. He wanted to know if she could hear the sounds that *he* had heard.)

"See those pines?"

She nodded.

"There're people living down there."

"Oh, there are not. Look at that moon!"

152

It *was* preternaturally large, albeit under a pox of some kind. Suddenly he attacked, tickling and lifting the woman, and then putting her on the ground. A very long while it had been since last he had stretched out on native ground, here where but recently the Creeks and Choctaw had carried out their slaughters. And if up north already it was turning cold, here everything was mild. He could interpret the moon in two different aspects, each in a separate eye. The woman…she had come a distance from *her* natal town. And now she was lying flat on her back and blinking up in wonder.

"Ah well," said Lee. "Oh very well, and so we'll go no further."

PART

III

Chapter Thirteen

THE SUN CAME UP ON AN AWFUL SCENE-THE HOUSE WAS IN VINES. He walked all around it three times, gawking at the damage, the objects in the yard, and the roof itself, so tattered and ragged it looked as if someone had been ploughing in it. Time, dread Time, Time which "turns men to dust," it had done its work again.

"Well!" said Lee. "The kindest thing would be to burn it."

"What?"

"Burn it."

He was surprised to see her run forward and throw herself into the house. Small was she, but not so small that she couldn't hold an armload of empty fruit jars fetched all the way from New York. Lee looked again. It was not fruit jars only; she had also a large green basket that he had twice thrown away in Pennsylvania, and more recently, had thrown away in South Carolina too.

He needed two hours to unload the car, and then another half-hour to choose a hiding place for the money, an exquisite location, perfect for its purpose—he would reveal it to no one—deep within the barn.

Of all his other buildings, only the smokehouse remained in reasonable condition. The crib and corn bin, the hen house and shop—these had been overgrown by a woods that he was disinclined to enter without his pistol. Instead, he climbed to the roof and stood there in some insecurity while he surveyed his whole demesne, from the quartz deposits to the north all the way down to where, even now, even at ten o'clock in the morning, a few occasional clouds of smoke were lifting from the valley. Closing his eyes, he strained to hear the sound of a door closing, hog grunting, child calling, rooster quibbling, and all the other manifold indications of a people living in secrecy on land that was officially *his*. To the west, he saw the wreck of a windmill, there where not so many years ago he used to look out over a civilization so much unlike this present one that it made him feel now like old Gregory of Tours gazing down sadly from his tower upon the ruined fields of Gaul.

And yet, he saw much that was good. The pond had *not* evaporated on him in his absence, not at all; he could see it gleaming bluely through the trees. The sun too had a redolence of its own, the aroma mixing with that of pines, plums, and honeysuckle. And yet, further, there was a dead grey highway with a convoy of snorting trucks on it, each truck driven by a lout—he knew them!—each lout facing eagerly to egregious Birmingham.

He came down sadly and then, drinking, began to drag items from the building—alien blankets, diseased mattress, obscene journals, defunct wasp nests, green basket, etc., etc., and made a pile of it in the orchard. *This* was how to inaugurate a new era—by setting a match to the whole last part of the late twentieth century. He danced, chortled, drank, and then, suddenly, spun to find a fat man standing just behind him. At once, Lee divined everything. The man was pale, ignorant, and had a red beard, but also carried an impressive string of catfish, one of them still thrashing. Lee's pistol lay in the second drawer of his grandmother's old-fashioned bureau.

"Shoo!" said Lee. "No, you'll just have to find other lodgings, most certainly you will. Sorry!"

The man said nothing. He seemed entranced by the fire. Or possibly it was its contents that amazed him. Lee decided to change his tack.

"Warm today, it is. And yet, soon, winter will be coming in. Hey! How's the football team doing this year?"

The man said nothing. Finally, he did turn at last and trudge off down the lane, disappearing into the brambles.

By noon, the house was free. Lee walked all through it, measuring for that library and scriptorium that he hoped to establish in the months to come. More than that, the place was highly defensible, given arms and ammunition and at least one fierce dog. Lee mused on it, finally getting down in the shooting position and aiming an imaginary rifle straight down the lane, which, however, tended to weave off toward the north-northwest before tapering down to a mere path. No one dare come that way, not if he treasured his life. Oddly, he could also sight down his "rifle" into the clouds, the sky, woods, past towns and crossroads and even (and this was the amazing part), even into the nation's largest city.

He went outside and, turning in the four directions, made a quick inventory of his lands and of the things that grew upon it. Trees, more than he could count; they offered with their noble bodies material enough to build him a rampart four miles high. And when he spun to look behind him, the house was still there too. According to his computation, he also owned two hundred and fifteen acres of sky, the clouds included—enough to cover his lands and, when night fell, entitling him to look up into his own private hoard of stars. And if he did not go so far as to claim the sun along with it, yet did he nevertheless insist upon the right to certain of its warmth. Winter was coming in. Lee drank. Yes, certainly it embarrassed him to be caught like this—an imaginary rifle over his shoulder and a true bottle in his mouth. The woman said nothing however.

In the afternoon they organized themselves for the trip to town, an adventure that worried him, based upon his remembrance of the place. Of the money—and he had to dig for it, and had too to cover it up again, scattering straw over the spot—of the money, he took only a tiny share, mostly in small bills. He did bring the revolver, fully loaded, hiding it under the dashboard of the car. The books he left behind, save only for a cheap edition in paperback of certain apothegms from the hand and mind of a certain once-famous French *encyclopédist*. It slipped in and out of his pocket as if the pocket had been stitched for it. (In actual fact, the stitching had been for Homer.)

They drove slowly, fearing to come too abruptly upon the mules and wagons that he still half expected to find behind each hill and rising. In his time, the fields had been busy with black people working the cotton; now, those same fields were stagnant, with not so much as a decent crop of weeds. They passed two doddering barns with doors and windows for mouths and eyes, one of them smiling and the other in tears. Came next a grove of hoary elms in various postures of agony, moss growing in their hair. Here, fifty years ago, a farm boy had hooked up a swing comprised of a rubber tire; now, the boy was gone and, no doubt, practicing unhappiness in egregious Birmingham.

There was much to see. Coming over the hill, he almost spoke out loud to find now one certain field that had turned to gingham against a sky of plaid. Here, too, love affairs had taken place, ignorance and passion, hostility between families, and the death of girls—the landscape had worn down almost to nothing beneath the burden of it. He saw an old man emerge from his cottage, and then stop and look up at the sky before turning suddenly and running back inside. Nearer, he saw four hogs in a pen, each gazing off luxuriously in its own favorite direction with smug expectations of the most pleasing kind. He saw a gander put one foot in the road, and then bravely turn and face the car. Further, a hart or hind (he did not know the distinction), or perhaps it was a roe, was feeding at the very edge of the meadow. Lee pointed to it, whereupon the thing stepped back suddenly into its kudzu mansion and slammed the door.

They passed a farmer in a truck. Lee did everything to get a look into his face, which proved dark and sunken and whiskered, and which turned away. Once there had been a feed store here; now, it had fallen in upon itself, establishing a ruin in which a numerous family of buzzards were dwelling in some dignity. Autumn possessed the Cahawba; here the colors were about as mellow as he had ever seen, straight "from the tube," as it were, and flecked with gilt. Again Lee felt that they were careening through the whorls and twists of some giant genius's aesthetic-craving mind. He saw a lake with a loon pinned to it, a cup of bright blue fluid, and behind that, the corduroy hills on which nothing would grow again, owing to so many broken love affairs.

He passed a cemetery where many of his own people lay unworriedly, quite apathetic now about the price of things. One grave was new—he saw a burst of bright flowers. To his thinking, nothing could be more beautiful than this: stainless sky, serene mules, music, and old hills worn down to a blueness with cilia for trees. There on the horizon indeed the beautifulness was more than could be endured, for which reason no one lived there anymore. As to how many farmers had come and gone, how many seasons… No one had written it down.

They entered town with extreme precaution. He was struck by the number of little colored houses jumbled up together and facing off indifferently in all various directions, as if here the people had no concern for symmetry, or for where the sun might rise, or for whether there was space enough for a person to squeeze between the homes. Lee marveled. He saw a pale girl with *two* babies, one large and one small, both bald. He did so love the rural poverty; to his notions, it offered the only genuine alternative to that potential high culture that America had long ago opted to eschew. Next, he saw three old men, dry ones, who sat turning slowly in unison at everything that passed. The world was old and they knew it, and, yes, they were old too; they knew it. Lee nodded in friendly fashion, a serious mistake that inspired them with alarm. Meanwhile, from somewhere there had come the smell of new-made bread, the intoxication of it mixing with pine, mimosa sap, and the bouquet of the nearby brown river with its mosses and eels. Suddenly, Lee stopped. There on the curb an eleven-year-old girl was dawdling and singing to herself while writing in the dust with a stick. Love—would any come her way? And life fulfill her fate?

At the gas station, they were attended by a large, smiling, blond-headed boy who displayed on his upper arm a most vivid tattoo-portrait of a certain famous football coach. Lee was delighted. He liked his ignorant people to be *truly* ignorant— may all things flow to their eternal extreme!—and liked it too that the boy had a huge honest belly that hung out over a snakeskin belt. Lee paid, shook hands with him, and then stood for a time expatiating about the weather.

"And the fishing—does it go well with you, the fishing?"

"Yes, sir; done good last week, real good."

"I'm pleased." Lee came nearer. He could see no guile anywhere, neither in the boy's face nor in his movements, nor in his clear blue and untroubled eyes. "I wouldn't advise it."

"Sir?"

"New York. Europe, too, it's just as rotten."

The boy nodded and blushed and then, suddenly, got down on his back and scooted up under the car in order to look at something. Lee waited a good three minutes for him, until he saw that the boy was not coming out again. Finally, lifting out his wife (she was reluctant to leave the shelter of the car), he guided her across the road, down past the welfare office and men's hairstylist, and then into a poorly lit hardware with a slowly revolving ceiling fan and two dangling coils bejeweled with the corpses of flies. They both needed some time to adjust to the obscurity, which, toward the rear, turned to outright nighttime conditions. Here, poised on a stool, there was a little man with straw hair who either had expired some years ago or else was so full of wisdom that he saw all and knew all, and wore a little smile. Judy never saw him; she was looking at the baskets and clay pottery, of which there was a quantity. She durst not touch anything however.

Lee worked his way yet further into the dark, into a region of seeds, tools, fishing equipment, and the like. Here, he detected the scent of linseed oil, most subtle of all known odors, also the gleam of hammers and axes that were newly minted and never yet used by any unsympathetic hand. Truly, he had an appreciation for tools and was anxious to possess himself of as many as he could, before their proper usage was forgotten by modern man. Suddenly, he unsheathed a saw from its cardboard scabbard and, lifting his glasses, inspected its teeth at close range. Wonderful instrumenta-tion—the Greeks would have been pleased. Next, he scooped up half a pound of screws, more valuable than diamonds, and allowed them to dribble through his fingers. Ingenious things, he considered them to represent the forward evolu-tion of the all-too-simple nail. Furthermore, they were easily to be stolen, albeit not in sufficient numbers as to be worthy of him. Instead, he served himself with two pounds each of bolts and nuts together with a mysterious little box holding number five fishhooks, each of them craftily manufactured, and each coated in a rainbow-hued film of number three oil. Ammunition! He pounced on it, opening several of the pack-ages until he hit upon his own favorite caliber, copper-headed beauties that would delight the very soul of his weapon now languishing in the glove compartment of the car. He weighed them individually, cradling them tenderly in the palm of his hand—three ounces each. Suddenly, he shivered violently, thinking of the effect these things could have upon a crowd, especially a crowd in New York, especially if the crowd were nude. He stole two boxes, the heaviness of them very nearly dragging off his trousers. He atoned for it by buying two fur-ther boxes with actual money. All this, bullets, ax, screws, and bolts—all of it he fetched up to the man at the counter who sat listening keenly to a radio program that, judging from it, had originated up north in the 1940s and only just now was emptying out upon Alabama.

"Charlie McCarthy! Ain't he something now?"

Lee grinned.

"Yes, sir, old Charlie. My, my. Now let's see what you got here: ax, yes, yes."

"And bullets too."

"'Cartridges,' we call 'em down here. Four boxes? Heavy, ain't they? So you're going to fix that place up then? My, my. Last we heard, you were still in South Carolina. Moving real slow."

"But…"

"New York girl?"

Lee admitted that she was. Just now she was standing in the aisle, her arms both heavy laden with pots and pans, candles, and a fleece blanket that appeared to have been stitched together out of a vast number of opossum skins.

"Winter's coming in," said Lee.

"Never realized how short they are, New York girls. Wonder what she looks like behind all that *fleece*? Watch it!"

Lee caught her. Together, they had over two hundred dollars of merchandise, most of it in the tools. The man added it slowly, using a pad and pencil and pausing once for the radio, and then once again to check Judy's face.

"Well!"

"You should have seen her when she was eighteen."

"Why, yes; I can picture it, even as I sit here."

Lee stepped forward, interposing himself. At first, he tried to pay with an antique coin, a gaudy thing, well burnished, with the portrait of an owl on it. At once, the man pushed it back at him. Lee was reduced to paying with bills, green ones that, as he watched ruefully, forever disappeared into the man's spade-like paw.

They carried the stuff to the car, secured it, and then ran across to the grocery where three women (one of them wearing a Sunday hat with two stuffed birds on it together with nest

and fledglings) had come together and were whispering excit-
edly about Judy. Lee came nearer. Truth was, he could remember this store down to this little brown dog's great-gran-
dam, who also used to slumber behind this same counter.
The candy, too, that used to keep him lying awake at night,
it was the same bright selection in the same glass compartment, saving only for what the roaches had carried away.
The grocer, too, a nervous type with a broom and apron—
they looked at each other across the space.

"How's the team doing this year?"

"I knew it was you. I didn't say anything, of course." He
went back to sweeping. Then: "O, I knew who it was, soon
as I seen him!"

Lee was shocked. Quickly he went through his memories
of all the people he had known. "I'm trying to think: Whom
did I know that…?"

The man waited.

"…that could turn out…"

"Like me? Hey, I wouldn't want you to think I was *always*
like this."

"No, no." He went forward to shake the man's hand. It
was dim in the building, the dust constituting a medium for
the morning light; nevertheless, Lee was beginning to discover
in this person that same wild little boy who used to be so
good at horses. They shook warmly, and then stepped back
to judge one another.

"You've been everywhere, I reckon."

Lee nodded. "Yes. Yes, I have. But it wasn't any good."

"Me, I've been here."

"Don't say that! It makes me envious."

"Education too—I can tell."

"Yes, some. Greeks, mostly."

"I'll be jiggered."

"Which is not to say that I've *entirely* ignored the modern
Europeans, no, no."

"Lord, no; nobody would say that."

"But *you*, do you still…?"

"I ain't been on a horse in twenty years."

"What!"

"I doubt there's five horses in the whole county."

"No!"

"They've left us, Leland, and they ain't coming back no more."

"No horses, no mules."

"*Nobody* raises cotton, not anymore."

Lee could feel his gorge rising. "No cotton, no grist mills. No wagons."

"Now, there *is* a grist mill. One."

"Oh?"

"They're using it for a nightclub."

"I see. Well maybe we ought to just go pay them a little visit, you want to? I've got a pistol."

The man grinned, but then grew morose again. "It's my son, Leland; he's managing it."

"The hell with him! Write him off, Harold, it's for the best. Why in Roman times, a man could kill a son that wasn't any good."

"Could?"

"Rome too however turned rotten—never forget that."

"It's the wife, Leland. She'd never let me do it."

"I see. Yes, well, if you're going to let *her* make the decisions… Me, *I* make the decisions in *my* family."

There was a hush, the three women glaring at him with eyes that bulged with hostility.

"Do?"

"Absolutely! You see *me* wearing an apron? Write him off, Harold; you should. Her too."

For a moment, he thought the man might actually weep. Suddenly, Lee spotted something he had not seen in so many years, he was not certain he was actually seeing it—a shelf loaded down with jars of black molasses. He flew to look at them more closely.

Each jar weighed two pounds. Smiling, he lifted one of them several times, finally forcing off the lid in order to whiff the divine smell. The grocer stood watching proudly.

"How is it, Leland?"

Lee now sampled it, finding the taste dark, dark as licorice, but also turbid, turbid as tar, and tinged with sulfur. "Stay!" Again he sniffed, pondered, and then suddenly brought it up and drank as if it were water. Judy was appalled.

"Lee!"

"The past is not entirely gone," said Lee finally, "no. Say rather that it has been gathered up and set aside momentarily into these jars."

"You think so?"

"Absolutely. Why, I can smell all the old things—honeysuckle and kerosene, and the wet smell of mules wet from wet rain."

"I'll be damned! I tell you what, Leland—how about if we just opened *all* these jars? Right now!"

"I'd like to. Amaze the world, it would! But we can't do it, Harold."

"I know."

"Because…"

"I know, I know." He drifted off, leaving Lee with the whole past arrayed in front of his eyes. It was a hard choice; finally he settled upon the bottle that held his own twelfth year, a time when the mules were gone already, but radio was in its prime. Further down, Judy was choosing among the potatoes, a studious process; she wanted only the best ones, even if the best ones were not terribly good. Lee went for the beans, unpretentious beings that could be prepared over a stove, needing no electricity. Though cheap, the bread was coarse, and full of unbroken kernels. Cheese, on the other hand, was dear; he found a cake of it, wheel-sized and the color of gold, the price having been somewhat knocked down owing to its great longevity. Red cabbage was on sale; indeed, they were all but giving it away. Onions! These were heart-shaped affairs and had many little clots of red earth still clinging in their tentacles. (He left it to Judy to select the appropriate flour, meal, shortening, coffee, oil, soda, and so forth.) Clearly, they were not to starve in this place, not with growing weather persisting all the way to November. He passed by the chewing tobacco, past the cookie barrel, past flower bulbs and past the licking salt to the place where he measured out two pecks of peanuts, and then another that had been boiling in brine. He bought a pocket knife. Finally, having paid for it all with a large bill, he turned to shake with Harold, who had fallen into despondency.

"We'll have to go fishing, Harold."

"You say that. It'll never happen."

"We might!"

"Never, never, never, never, never."

"You won't even shake hands?"

"And I was doing real well this morning."

Lee nodded sadly. "In future, I'll send my wife."

"Might be best."

"That way…"

"Right."

Now he shook. They could not, however, look one another in the eye.

They crossed the square, passing in the shade of the one-armed Confederate statue whose face was largely eaten away with suffering and rust. Here was a fountain with a cool green froth on it, and with numbers of giant goldfish flashing in the depths. A black woman was sitting on a bench, shelling peas in the center of town. Lee was taken aback by the number of bearded philosophers speculating up and down the sidewalk, mere tramps, most of them. But he could not deceive himself for long—here too the people had been inseminated by television and junk "music," and everywhere he looked the feminine principle was in the ascendancy, and men wore looks of guilt. He saw one, a middle-aged man who was pulling faces and making noises that, thirty years ago, would have been considered idiotic. Next came a car in which four new-style youths, extraordinarily well dressed (one had a briefcase), seemed to be rehearsing the roles of bankers and CEOs. Too late, Judy tried to call his attention instead to the blue hills that lifted above the western levee.

"Too late," he said, "I see 'em. And just look at that!" (It was a daffy-looking girl, a gum-chewer whose lustrous face was smeared over not just with television and not just with "music." She had also been trained in self-esteem.)

The liquor shop, when they came to it, proved to be a low-ceilinged building, wonderfully supplied. He could not help but notice however that so many of the bottles were but simple old-fashioned fruit jars that bore no labeling of any kind. He ordered twelve brandies, adding four more, an action that brought down more attention on him than he wanted. The place served also as the post office and was jammed with people, leathery types with pocket watches who stood viewing him (and his wife) with silent regard. Lee hummed. He was beginning to feel that feeling he had felt before, namely that these men would certainly turn and rend him, as soon as they knew what he was thinking.

He desired to open the first of the brandies on the spot; instead, he hoisted the supplies and marched back straightway to the courthouse. He had not been in town two hours and already he (and his wife especially) were the topic on every tongue. He saw two women pointing and giggling and ex-changing comments about…what? That he had come flying home with his tail between his legs? No. They did not know it was home, did not know him, and had *never* known her. He bowed, sweepingly. Another ten minutes and he would have offended *everyone*.

They drove slowly through increasing poverty toward those low blue hills that hemmed in the town on the western side. The road was of sand, the way dangerous, and the unpainted shacks, which lined both sides, were in such poor condition that he could at times see through chinks in the walls, finding here an old woman rocking in front of a fire, there a child playing with toys. His heart leapt up in joy: poverty! This, to him, was humankind's ordained station, and the one most propitious for spiritual development. Fortunately, they were sitting out on their porches where Lee could see them, whole families indeed. He slowed in order to look them over, finally coming to a halt in front of a pine cabin with a blond-headed man—utter trash, as he seemed to Lee—sitting on the steps sharpening his saw.

"Oh! Oh! Oh!" said Lee. "Give me but twelve more like that, and we could take the whole city of New York!"

"He's looking."

"And me, I'm looking too."

The cabins had eyes; nevertheless, Lee got out lazily, in southern style, pausing to light a cigarette with his hand cupped against the wind.

"Winter's coming in! No, actually it's been following me all the way from New York."

The man nodded once, and then squinted off into the windy north from whence Lee had said that he had come. "New York, yes sir; I knew I'd seen that car *somewhere*."

"Been there, have you?"

"You might say that. Served two years upstate."

"Two!" (He seated himself languorously on the upper step. The man was willing to accept a cigarette—a good sign—and willing to shake hands as well.) "Two years. That's a long time for people like you and me."

"Till I got me a smart lawyer."

"New York's full of lawyers."

"Full of lots of things."

They chuckled both, both squinting ruggedly into the wind that twined between the cabins and was the cause of the neighbors wearing blankets around their shoulders.

"Pefley's my name."

"Pefley. You ain't kin to old C.T., I don't reckon?"

"Very probably. But I've been away so long, you understand, and so much has happened that…"

"C.T.'s dead."

"No!"

"Found him sitting in his chair—you know that old red chair of his—sitting there looking at the television. Dead."

Lee groaned. It made him uncomfortable that a crowd of children, barefooted in spite of the weather, had clustered around the car and were poking at Judy.

"My wife," said Lee.

"Well hell, ask her to come on in. Y'all want some brew?"

"She's from New York."

"That don't make no never-mind to me." He rose exhaustedly and went inside, leaving Lee to go and fetch his wife, who came gladly now. But she was slow to shake the man's hand, owing to the unseemly tattoos that adorned his upper forearm—reluctant too to drink the brew that was offered in a coffee cup. Lee drank off his immediately and then held out the cup for more. The man had not needed twenty seconds to get a fire going, a great green and yellow blaze nourished on pine. And in fact, the cabin was squeezed tight with firewood, including at least two cords worth of well-seasoned hickory and oak. Lee explained it this way to Judy:

"He's saving the hardwoods for January."

She nodded. The table itself was unsanitary, with a slab of bacon on it, a knife, several shotgun shells rolling about at will, and two video cassettes, of which one had come unspooled. Lee also detected evidence of women's clothing hanging over the door—a slip and an old-fashioned print dress that seemed to date from the 1940s. The women, the places, the sentences this man had served—just now he was squatting before the fire, lost in speculation and smoke.

"I don't know," said Lee. "Maybe I shouldn't have left here in the first place. Well! Except to marry Judy, I mean. And then I should have come running back home with her—

she was the only thing they had that was any good—and spent the rest of my days in a wretched little cabin like this one. Why, I could have been an interesting person too, instead of… Insurance! What do *I* have to do with insurance? Public relations. I don't even *like* public relations. Consultancy. You ever done any consultancy?" (The man shook his head sadly.) "Mutual funds?"

"Now you talk about the army—that's where *I* went bad."

"Eight million people, eight! All of them crammed into a couple hundred acres."

"I know it. And some of them fellers never been fishing in their whole lives."

"And the women…"

"Whores. All whores. All. No, not *you*, ma'am. *Them*."

"Whores, taxes, insurance."

"We had one of them tax fellows. He come down here just looking for trouble."

"Oh?"

"Yeah. But we won't be having any more problems with *him*, oh no, no, no." He grinned. There were numbers of pelts tacked to the wall, of which Lee could identify most of them, if not all.

"More 'brew,' please."

"Old C.T., *he* liked my brew."

"Old C.T. Dead! Hard to believe. Wonder if any more of my people are up in those hills?"

The man twisted, looking at him in surprise. "Why, shore! There's Floyd, he's not dead. There's Mabel. Why shoot, there's lots of 'em up there. And Aunt Lulu too."

"Good Lord! Still alive? The one that used to cook?"

"*Still* cooks. Best cook in this part of the county. And got all them ribbons to prove it too."

"Good Lord! Lulu. Why, I must…"

"Go see her, you bet."

"Cooks?"

"Whew!"

He woke three times during the night, once in order to rise and to rediscover that he was sleeping in the criminal's cabin, and then once again to rearrange the bed. The sheets had *not* been ironed, not in a very long time, nor were they imbrued with that mildew and camphor smell that Lee insisted upon when he was in the South. Moreover, it was his habit to put on his glasses at certain hours and to make certain it really was his own pretty wife lying at his side.

The third time he awoke, he went outside. The night was chill, winter coming in. Across the way, a young girl had come out onto the porch with her two babies and, while singing, was fueling each of them on a different breast.

Someday this whole village, poverty and people, someday it would be nothing more than hints and suggestions in old history books. He looked toward distant Birmingham, finding it aglow at one moment, and then again, darker than before. These were strange doings, nights in Alabama; in the adjoining yard he saw a hog, its face a study in rapture, the result of too many hours of theorizing on the stars. The gate itself was down, and now Lee saw others of them (hogs) leaving town and moving noiselessly out onto the broad black swatch of field, where they hoped to find freedom at last. Normally, Lee cheered for the farmers; this time, his heart was with the hogs.

He returned to bed and lay for a while looking into his wife's face from half an inch away. Finally, carefully, he tried to lift her nearer lid, finding it heavy, or rather, that is to say, finding it resolute. And then, too, he must not disturb the criminal, an uneasy sleeper indeed, judging by the snorts and popping sounds that came every few seconds from the next room.

Lee was himself the very poorest sleeper in the world. Memories of literature came to mind, to be quickly followed by certain old-world opera tunes that would someday finally drive him completely insane. Music and drink, the Alabama sky and Judy slumbering divinely at his side—he should be happy now, save only for the lack of one further thing. But he did not know what it was.

Chapter Fourteen

GRITS, HAM, BUTTERMILK, COFFEE WITH SOOT IN IT—LEE'S WIFE HAD NEVER HAD SUCH A BREAKFAST, SO COMPLETE, OR SO EARLY IN THE MORNING. The two men watched while she sampled delicately before finally electing to surrender to it. She had put on her cheery red sweater, and the tip of her nose was cheery too. Winter was coming in, wherefore the three of them lingered somewhat too long at the fire, reluctant to leave it.

"Well," said Lee.

The host nodded. Bad dreams had bothered him all night—it might almost be better to be a real insomniac, like Lee—and now he sat gazing with horrible fixation into the devilish flames. His complexion was unhealthy, and his long blond hair needed to be washed.

"Well," said Lee. "We ought to leave now."

The man agreed. Already a party of farmers (carrying nets) had passed by in the road. Evidently, they meant to track down the hogs, and just as evidently, the host wanted to join them.

"Well." Lee rose and shook with him, but knew better than to offer money. Instead, he ambled to the car and cut off a good two-or three-pound wedge of yellow cheese, wrapping it in a page of newspaper. This the man accepted.

"See them trees? Where them pines is swaying up on Mahler's Nose? *That's* where she lives. But you want to be real careful."

"I always want it."

"'Cause otherwise, you might get shot."

"Right."

"Now when you get close, you need to tell 'em who you are."

"Tell 'em."

"'Cause otherwise... Know what I'm saying? Now I recommend you let your wife go first. They won't shoot her."

Lee noted it down.

It was a bright, clear, clean, cheerful morning, sparkling on the surface and sparkling to the soul. One single childish cloud, tiny as a colt, was galloping this way and that, never finding its mother. Lee set out in high spirits, his breakfast and his four days of beard giving him to believe that he had acculturated already and now belonged to this place. And if he was good at driving in sand, it was from twenty years of driving in snow. He passed a troupe of black farmers with hoes over their shoulders, among them a dazzling albino whose gaze betrayed a high intelligence joined by the cruel God to a startling shape. Inside, the car was cozy, full of music and books, while here *outside*, the rough world was furnished in telephone poles, broken pines, and a soft road that yielded beneath them and threatened to toss them off into the gully. Very little cotton to be seen—the nineteenth century had waned away at last, even if it had needed the entire twentieth to get it done. Instead, he spotted a few paltry attempts at soybeans and sorghum, some mediocre cattle, and then a spate of suntan salons and video rentals operating out of former churches. He passed a shopping mall crowded with youths, each youth wearing earphones and a T-shirt with a slogan on it.

He wanted to weep; instead, he turned the music higher, as if he might overwhelm the evil sights with lovely sounds. And then, by driving up into the hills, he hoped to come into a place where there were better things to look upon.

His heart was beating wildly, he who had imagined that all his people were extinct by this time, or at any rate too far scattered ever to be found again. He saw a collapsed barn, an old-style structure that had been joined together with pegs and notchings in the antique fashion. He slowed, finally stopping and getting out and going over (marching through the briars), in order to specify whether the work had not been done by one of his own gloomy forebears, silent men remembered for having been good with adzes. The sun was sprinkling down brightly, grainy rays that lay among the timbers. He saw a lizard, a grey one whose anguished eyes told that these ruins were his, his alone, but that he had no good way to defend them. At one time this barn, when whole and upright, it had sheltered all manner of ungulates and kine, mules and horses, all of them very glad to have been given such a hotel in which to wait out the horrible nights. Lee sat, mulling upon one of the shingles, an inch-thick slice so brave and stalwart that not even a hundred years had sufficed to make it curl or rot. His thoughts turned again to old Hesiod, the poet of the full barn and good workmanship. Soon, however, his mind turned to yet other things.

It turned to winter. Now, taking his wife by the hand, he strolled with her down to the rather lassitudinous pond that was so stained with oxides that it resembled red wine.

"And here," he said, "here is where an old-world couple lay together once, bringing forth all those men and women who gave rise to the people that brought forth *me*."

She looked at it, a cozy nook comprised of vines. Lee felt suddenly a great wish to see his wife bathing in the wine; instead, he said: "Why, we could be looking down upon their love play even now, except for one thing only—the passing of a certain duration of thin, water-colored Time. Otherwise, they'd be loving still."

She looked at it. Above, a crow was moving back and forth slowly, showing more interest in them than Lee liked to see. He went on talking however:

"And *there*, there there used to be a mill. See? Why, you can still make out one of the blades, a 'spoon,' as it were, huge and capacious, and as if planted in the ground."

She marveled. They had climbed to no very great elevation and yet, behind them, they could see both the existing town (smoke coming from the factories), and also the shadow of its predecessor community, now abandoned, that had been situated some two miles toward the north-northeast. Further still was the cemetery with its many dozens of gravestones that looked like teeth. And then, of course, the levee which served in lieu of a wall. (Lee saw a small black boy riding exuberantly along the crest of it in a dog-pulled cart.) Beyond that, there was nothing, uninhabitable terrain where *no one* ventured (apart from one or two unbalanced women in the town who might still go forth from time to time in search of herbs). As for the levee builders themselves, a remote people who had been proud enough to engrave their outlandish-sounding names on the escarpment… Lee had nothing but gratitude for them. Their work had *not* been perfect however, no, and he could see very plainly where on that dreadful day the perimeter had fallen in upon itself, there where the enemy had come pouring through in jubilant numbers—he did not like to think about it. He slumped back to the car in a dark mood and started the engine.

The mountain was littered with evidences of the era that was over. He spied the rim and the spokes of a wagon wheel, though he could not conceive how any animal could have pulled such a vehicle to this level. Driving higher, he began to make out the faint, far-distant spumes of the almost-dead volcanoes that had emptied the adjoining county of all its people. Shielding his eyes, he began to understand too how it was precisely *there*, there inside volcanoes, that clouds were built.

They went on, urging the car forward. The road itself had funneled down to a mere trail, and soon enough they came to a spot where two pines, touching at waist and shoulders, forbad them to proceed further.

"Well!" (said Lee.) "We've come this far."

"I know."

"And up yonder, I suppose…"

"What will they do to us, Lee?"

He shrugged, took up the pistol and loaded it, but then put it back. In his pocket he had a copy of Lucretius, a British imprint in flexible bindings; it protruded a good four inches into the light. The other pocket carried a stock certificate, a knife, and a tin of unopened sardines.

The way now became more difficult, especially for the woman, whose thin feet were not well designed for stepping through the hills. Moreover, the path was unfriendly; they came almost at once to that wagon itself whose missing wheel Lee had discovered on a lower level; apparently it been set across the trail to keep people from coming further.

"Hmm," said Lee. "One must assume that…"

"Please, Lee. Let's go back."

"No doubt this is all calculated to keep tramps and peddlers at bay. No, I can understand that."

"Please."

They inched forward. The second obstacle consisted in just this: the trail itself ended. They found themselves probing into the underbrush, hands held out to defend themselves against the briars. Lee drank. He knew enough to keep a keen watch for traps and snares, and enough also to pause every few steps to verify the lay of the land and position of the sun. He saw no wildlife of any kind, excepting only one late grasshopper who sat chewing cynically and spitting out what looked like brown tobacco juice.

They considered themselves lost. Very glad was he, and gladder still was Judy, when they pushed finally into an open space that at least allowed them to see the sky again. She knew so little about woods, Judy; for the third time, Lee began to worry about having snatched her away so abruptly from her native New York. He flew to her side, continuing to shelter and to comfort her even as the man—he had a shotgun across his knees and was sitting on a log—even as the man began to put his questions.

"Now just what in the goddamn hell…?"

"Lee," said Lee. "No, it's alright; I'm a Pefley too."

"What?"

"Pefley."

"Goddamn IRS man, is what you are."

"Ha! IRS. No, no, I…"

"See that stick lying there on the ground?"

"Yes," said Lee. "Yes I do." (He reached down tenderly and touched it.)

"Good. Now whatever comes across that stick—and I don't much care whether it's an elbow, or a knee, or a foot—whatever it is, it gets blowed off."

Lee jumped back. He had been striving to examine the man's face, to find whether it had the family features in it. "Are *you* a Pefley? No, I only ask." That was when he spied a second person, a tall, lank youth, thin as the very slender pine he was trying to hide behind. Other pines had yet others hiding behind them.

"*She* can come," said the first man. "*You* can't."

"Now just hold on there a minute! Do you have *any* real notion of who I am? No." He stepped forward, whereupon the youth yelled out in wild alarm:

"Watch it! He's got a book with him!"

Lee jumped back. Further up the hill a woman (she was holding a calf by the collar) was watching worriedly. Lee believed that he could also see the home as well, although it blended so with the hill, and had a turfen roof… He could not be sure. Finally, he cleared his throat and spoke out loud and plain:

"Never, never would I have returned so far, coming all this way, had I not cause to think that we contain some of the same gene cells, you and me. Yes, and have seen the same old photographs too."

"He talks funny."

"He's on the wrong side of that stick too."

"Look at me! The nose, etc. Clearly, we…" He stopped. It disappointed him that Judy had turned and was trudging back sadly in the general direction of the car. "Judy!"

"That how you talk to your woman? Screaming?"

"No, no, I…"

"*We* don't do that, Pefleys don't, talk to their women like that."

"Morin did." (This in a thin voice from behind one of the pines.)

"Morin. That will be Lulu's grandfather on her mother's side—am I right?"

There was a shocked silence, the man and boy and the three half-visible figures among the trees glancing toward each other in surprise.

"Shoot, you probably just *read* that somewhere. In a book. Besides! Who authorized *you* to come up here and talk about Lulu, hm? Why, she might be dead, for all you know."

"But she's not. Is she?"

"Damn!"

(He had been moving forward gently, until now he was on a plane with the others. One courageous move and he might actually be able to deprive the man of his gun. He decided not to try it. Instead, inclining first toward the boy and then to one of the pines, he tried to read whether the family features shone brightly or weakly, and whether the late twentieth century had reached this far up the hills.)

"I brought presents."

"We don't want 'em."

"But I left them in the car."

It was steep going. A ram or goat of some species—this too wearing a collar with spikes on it—stood aside for them. Even here, directly in front of the house, it was difficult to discriminate between the sod roof and the encompassing terrain. He imagined that he could also read some of the family features in the extreme perfectionism of the structure, the garden, the well-combed animals. As to the family dog, he and Lee immediately recognized in each other the family traits.

"He'll slobber all over you, if you let him. Mordecai!"

They moved into the immense hallway decorated with rifles on the wall. Instead of books, Lee saw hoards of ammunition, boxes of it piled up very tidily on the shelves and mantel and, he did not doubt, in the closet too. He looked for, and found, the great portrait of his own grandfather, a furious-looking man in a frame of inch-thick planks.

"A great man," said Lee solemnly, stationing himself in front of the picture.

"Yup. Never got much sleep though, they say. I'm Abner."

Now, finally, they shook, doing it under the gaze of the family's progenitor. Lee also turned and shook with the boy, whose hand, although it seemed to have great strength in it, was kept under strict control. Lee's eye meantime ran up and down the exposed electrical wiring that followed the joists and beams, even unto the kitchen, where, Lee had to suppose, Lulu was being diligent. He listened for, and once

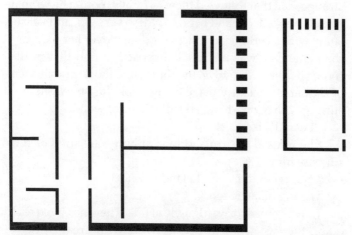

did hear, the clash of pans. And that was when he caught a momentary glimpse from the window, a superb view, dumbfounding in its impact, of the gorgeous sky and valley.

"O!" he said. "A view like that! No wonder you defend this spot in the way that you do, a view like that!"

Both man and boy blushed with pleasure. Himself, Lee crowded to the pane, pressing at it, awed by the colors and the depth, and by the languid volcanoes whose last feeble utterances so far away on the horizon gave proof that they were coming down to the end of their cycles. "Who needs books!" And then: "Is *this* where I was born?"

"Shorely. And then you went away."

Lee blushed. "I was young. I wanted…"

"We know what you wanted." They looked to Judy, who had gone up to the window and was standing shyly, like a child, with her hands behind her back. From the kitchen, Lee could hear a pan dancing on the stove.

"I'm ready to see Lulu now."

He was brought back through a long dark hall stacked on both sides with excellent-looking firewood, hardwoods all, that filled the space from floor to ceiling and left only a narrow thoroughfare for Judy and for Lee, and for the two strange men that followed them to Lulu's room. The woman herself was old, old and bent, so old, so very old, and yet she stood with a certain jauntiness, lording it over her tools and the flame. Lee was not at all surprised to find that in this room all things, the stove, the churn, and the flour mill, were of the same ancient vintage as the cook. Just now, she was stirring with a long-handled ladle made of wood.

"Leland's back."

She refused to turn and look at him—this too failed to surprise him.

"No," she said. "No, Leland's gone."

"Brung his wife too."

Judy stepped forward, shyly at first. They measured each other, the two women. Lee watched with great pride as slowly and slowly it sank in upon the old woman that here was a resolute wife who, although she might indeed derive from out of the cold north, yet was more resolute and more self-contained, not to mention quite lovely... Three times, the old woman looked her up and down.

"Why, I've got a granddaughter that's shorter than that! Or I used to anyway, before she run off to be a facilitator."

"Facilitator?"

"Yep," said Abner with pride, "they're trying real hard to get in touch with their true feelings down there. Assertiveness lab, don't you know."

"Ah!"

"Leland, too, he run off. Long time ago."

"But now I'm here."

"He'll come back someday."

"I'm back *now*."

"Shore," said Abner. "He'll come back. *With his tail between his legs!*"

They all laughed merrily, even Lulu, whose voice had that stuttering quality of a pan dancing on flames.

"I wanted..."

"She knows what you wanted."

"But if he *do* come back, you tell him to keep out of my kitchen, hear?"

Lee fled.

They gathered in the afternoon, the men did, in order to try the fishing in that thin wine-red pond that lay over against the cliffs. But this time, Judy remained behind in the kitchen, where, Lee divined, she was learning many more things than just cooking techniques alone.

The pond, once they had settled around it at elbow's length from each other, was narrow but deep, deep but thin, so deep, so narrow, and so tenuous indeed that he could *see* (even if he could yet snare) whole schools of particolored fish that liked to fly up near to the surface and preen in the sun. Finally he reached out, as if to scratch one of the things on the nose. Abner was aghast.

"Watch it, Leward! You'll lose your finger that way, you

sure as hell will." Then, after a moment: "Now I'm not trying to be *inhospitable*, you understand."

"I've got a pistol."

"No. No, that's against the regulations. And they know it too."

They all settled back for a long wait. His cousins, six of them, together with an old man, had come out from the woods where they had hidden and, nodding courteously, had seated themselves timidly at various points about the lake. One man wore bandages about his head, another was in bib overalls, and yet a third had brought his modem with him and was tinkering with it in his lap. These men, those of them that were actually fishing and not just watching Lee, they had dropped their lines to a much greater depth in the water, where, from moment to moment, it was possible to catch glimpses of a more noble species, brown trouts grazing in the columns of light. It was these, and never the gaudy ones, that Lulu required for her dinners. Lee's own bait was a mere worm, a suffering creature that had never done evil to *him;* nevertheless, he lowered it into the mob of dotted fish that populated, and indeed overpopulated, the cloudy depths. Ten minutes went by, Lee's mood turning gloomy. Three crows passed overhead, amused to see so many men wasting their time. Finally, drinking, Lee uttered what was on his mind:

"Europe's rotten too."

"Hm?"

"Rotten."

"Do tell!"

"Certainly. But it started *here*. No, no, not *here*" (he pointed into the lake), "not in Alabama. It started, and I say this without pleasure, it started in New York."

"New York! He's been there, you understand."

"Tell him to talk louder. Can't hear, way over here."

"New York!" said Lee, cupping his hands and exerting himself. "And all big cities. *That's* where it started. Television,

subways, and these great hecatombs of mules. Why, it'll soon
be illegal to think thoughts or to read books!"

"Got to have *some* rules, Leward."

Lee groaned. He had been feeding upon the gorgeous
view, all save that cement monument, larger than the Sphinx,
that one of the farmers had put up in the valley as a protest
against western imperialism. He coughed, and then went on:

"Let all those who are not reactionaries, let them go out
of the South, and let them not come back! Even here among
us now, there's a man with a modem in his lap. No! I want
me a world where *everyone* will know the wet smell of a wet
mule in wet rain." (He knew that he was getting excited. Knew
too that the old man especially was listening with increasing
respect—they looked at each other. Now, laying aside the
pole, Lee stood and stretched forth his arm over the waters.)

"As in Morin's time."

"Amen."

"*Everyone* poor, and no cities anywhere beneath the
goddamn sun!"

"*Now* he's talking."

"A *new* Civil War—this time we win!"

"Hee!" The boy too stood, clapping his hands. Abner
was smiling. Lee drank.

"Oh, I don't say it'll be easy."

"Hard, it's going to be hard."

"First, we have 'pick up' these cities—yes, I know they're
heavy—and set them down again—Atlanta, the egregious
Birmingham—set them down in…"

"New York!" cried Abner.

Lee was overjoyed with him. "Why, yes; no one will even
notice them there! New Orleans too."

"Macon!" said the tall boy.

Lee had to laugh; the suggestions that followed were
simply too fast to write down. "Yazoo!" he heard, and then
down to tiny "Brent!" Finally he put a stop to it:

"Well, but we'll need *some* towns at least, an entrepôt

here and there, to manufacture arms."

"Arms. I got a nephew works at the nuclear plant."

It was a good moment, nuclear, but soon they all fell silent and morose again. The fish were shrewd, cynical even, and much too choosy for worms. Finally, after a blank period of perhaps twenty minutes, the old one loaded his little box of tackle and then turned and trundled off down the hill. It was one of the young ones who asked:

"Leward?"

"Yes?"

"Tell us about the women."

"Women?"

"New York women."

"There are no women."

"Say what!"

"I got the last one myself. No, the women have all turned to men now. Sorry."

"I hate to hear that, Leward, I just hate it. I was thinking: Maybe *I* might want to get *me* a woman, like you done."

"You haven't heard the worst."

"Worst!"

"The men—you haven't heard what *they've* turned into."

There was a long difficult silence as the men looked to one another in a sort of alert sorrowfulness.

"Men unto women, women unto slime, slime unto slime in thousand-dollar suits; they be like nothing so much in this earth as these poisoned 'gaud fish' that fritter here in the shallows. Oh God, would that I had my pistol just now!"

"Kill 'em all!"

"And yet, and yet, and yet. This was once a country that might almost have taken up where the Greeks left off. And where, gentlemen, where is the American High Culture *now*?"

Wade shrugged. "Gone?"

"Not gone," said Lee. "Not begun."

He saw that he had succeeded in depressing them, the

fartherest thing from his wish. To cheer them, he began humming. And that, of course, was when one of the trash fish, a box-shaped creature, bright orange in color and endowed with very long eyelashes, took his worm, his line and sinker, and tried to take *him*. It was a mistake to lift the thing from the water; at once, it began spurting off in all directions, a keen stream of poison that sent the fishermen reeling back from the shore, not indeed with "rebel yells," but nasal tones of pure dismay. Lee was disappointed. The fish and he, they looked at one another. With no pistol, no harpoon, he was trying, uselessly, to drown the thing in its own native milieu.

They collected in the kitchen. The family had more surviving members than Lee had supposed; he found himself seated across from a shriveled woman who held in her lap a giant pale baby that looked like a ventriloquist's dummy. Wade, as it proved, already had a wife. She did not, however, have the family features, nor did she wear the authentic look and expression of someone who had been raised up in Calauria County. And meanwhile, next to her, there was a fat woman in a hat who had learned to hum religious hymns even while she went on feeding.

"Oh, he was evil," said Lulu, "Leland was. He used to live here, don't you know."

"But now I'm back."

"God knows where he is now."

They brought out the chicken pie, a savory dish, the meat plump and softened and with some of the original bones sticking out. Lee delved into it, deep, deep. But his eye, *that* was upon the little delicate pink glass dish that held its own fund of watermelon rind pickles. He had to go back over his memories, years of them, and thousands of nights, in order to identify what it was.

"Watermelon pickles!"

"Up north, I reckon. I don't guess we'll ever know why he left."

Came the biscuits, greater than dumplings; Lee opened one of them, forcing into its maw a wedge of true butter—immediately, it began to melt—and then following it with several dosages of bright green jelly.

"Jelly!" said he. "Jelly made from quinces." Then: "Look at Judy."

She blushed. Never a tremendous eater, she had now been caught out in the open with a biscuit in one hand and cornbread in the other. As for those lips he had kissed a million times, they were all besmirched in buttermilk now. And that was when he saw the plump brown trouts his great-granduncle had caught—each trout held a boiled partridge in its mouth.

"Trouts too!"

"Just enjoy it, Leland. We can *talk* about it later."

They all now bent over their work. It was a serious time and yet already he had espied, and had smelled, the coming of the odor of the hot blueberries steeped in ice cream.

"Jesus!"

"That's northern talk, Leward. We don't say that."

He hushed. Across from him, the dummy was drunk on iced tea. Lulu allowed one more glass of it, and then began swatting at the child with her long-handled spoon.

It was true, he had to admit it, this was the best homecoming ever. Finally, he pushed back and loosened his belt. Winter was coming and already one of the cousins had started a blaze, a small one, in the enormity of the enormous fireplace. Now came Judy, pouring the mulberry wine.

"Try it!" she said. "It's good!"

"Yes. Apparently you've had quite a little bit already."

"Now Leward…" (Abner talking.)

"Yes?"

"I was thinking: what is he going to do with himself? Now that you're back, I mean."

"Why, he can stay right here!" said the little old man

with the glittering eyes, the same little old man who had been sojourning at the lake.

"Well…" said Lee. "I've got enough for four more years. And then…"

"Enough cash?"

"No, books. And then, I figure I could *always* go into mutual funds."

There was a long, painful silence. Having made the meal, Lulu was casting about for someone else to clear the table. One of the dogs came up, a great hairy item named "Glam." It was Glam that wanted the table.

"Or insurance," Lee went on. "Or, I could offer classes, yes. The Schopenhauer-Wagner-Nietzsche connection— now *that* should set this whole county alight!" He laughed, uproariously so—the wine was strong—until he saw that he was laughing alone.

"He could be a preacher," said Clarence.

"No, no, Leland's not a Mexican, never was."

"Mexican!"

"Affirmative Action, don't you know. Or leastwise, he wasn't no Mexican the last time *I* seen him."

That was true; there was another long, painful silence. Finally, after a few moments of thought, Lee said quietly:

"Donne was a preacher. And there's a very good one in *Moby Dick*."

"Well that's settled then. But where is he going to *live?*"

"Live here!" said the old man. "*I* got room!"

"I plan," said Lee, sipping at the wine, "I plan to live in the house that has come down to me through inheritance."

"Oh Lordy, you can't live *there*. No roof!"

Lee opened his mouth to talk, but was interrupted by a bearded man—Lee had not seen him before—coming awake in the corner.

"We got no mutual funds here in this county, no sir!"

Now Virgil spoke up: "That old place, it's got better than a hundred acres. Shoot, he could *take it out of cultivation*, you understand me? Get paid for it too."

"He's got a point."

"He's got no point! That land ain't *in* cultivation. He can't take it *out* if it ain't *in*."

"It's in," said Lulu. "I'm saying it's in." She surveyed the room, finding no one to gainsay her.

"Well that's settled. He's got his land, got his car, got his..."

"Pistol."

"...and got his reading material too."

Judy drank. Looking at her from across the room, Lee saw that she was adjusting to Alabama very well. She had land now, had books and wine and Glam's ugly head resting in her lap. More than that, she had Willard on one side (sleeping), and Greenlee (from whom Lee's own name had been inspired) on the other. And above, there still hung the massy portrait of the grandfather of them all, a man said to have been short in stature but tall, very tall, perhaps *too* tall and *too* fastidious in moral evolution. And all in all, Lee would have said that the room contained fourteen persons in it, exclusive of those billions of the dead who, it seemed to him just now, were pressing at the windows and gazing in hungrily at the few fortunate well-fed and still-living ones.

He woke, of course, long before morning came. It needed all his will to separate from the quilts and their smell, and from the arms of his dormant wife. He had to tread carefully, too, the house being full of people. One man indeed had taken out his teeth and was sleeping with them resting on his chest. Lee was surprised to find a sentry at the door, a tall man with the family features; they nodded to each other.

"Thought I'd step outside," said Lee, somewhat apologetically. "Have a smoke."

"Don't piss in the flowers. Lulu don't like that."

"Take a breath of fresh air."

"Shore. Winter's coming in."

In fact, he soon stepped off the porch and down into the

woods where there were no flowers but the wild ones. The valley was sparkling, even at this late hour; he saw an airplane come down close, as if for a landing, and then change its mind and go away. Of fireflies, Lee saw one only, the last of the season, whereas of *neon*, there were at least three still-flickering advertising signs left over from an earlier period. One was green, and shone greenly through the forest. Here Lee sat, smoking. He feared nothing, unless it were the snakes that, however, based upon what he remembered, very seldom went abroad at night. Instead, he waited upon the first of the raccoons. (For he knew well how irresistible to them was the glow of a cigarette, and how it worked upon their curiosity.) That glow, it was *not* enough to let him read. Nor did the stars and neon come to his assistance, nor had he made any attempt to smuggle reading material past the sentry. Suddenly, he grabbed for the pistol and the brandy, finding the former missing and the latter having turned to wine. That was when he snapped his fingers, smote himself on the forehead, and exclaimed out loud—among it all, he had forgotten to piss!

What, really, were they doing just now in New York? He rolled onto his belly and began sniffing of the good, strength-giving, red-clay earth. He was not a devout man; nevertheless, he found himself sending up a beseechment to the cruel God, begging Him to be cruel once more, cruel to New York, to permit the buildings to fall, tides to overlap the dikes, and subways to be filled suddenly with awful gases. In fact, he went further than that, asking for the ink to disappear from off the bonds and certificates of stock (!), and for every computer disc in town to be found neutralized by morning. He rolled, yearning for it, weeping, his face a dreadful study in the light of the bilious moon. "O Cruelty!" (he cried.) "Ye who up to now has loved only fortunate people, be cruel once more!"

Two lights came on in the house. Lee had begun to search in his coat with some panic, looking for the wine. And if he flattered himself that it really was the cruel God coming toward him to give heed... No, it was merely the first of the raccoons, a tentative creature, very bashful, a thrall to curiosity.

In the morning, Lee and his wife packed up their few things—the nuts and food and the several rather small articles that Lee had chosen to keep without discussion. In turn, he offered up his sole copy of Lucretius, a gift which seemed rather to offend Lulu than to please her. Himself, he wanted nothing whatsoever to do with Glam's puppies. Judy took two, the ugliest.

"Leland, now, when he used to live here…"

"I'm right here!"

"…before he got so *grand*. Books, you understand."

Judy shook hands with her graciously, thanking her for all things, and for the puppies. Abner had gone off early, taking his pruning fork with him. Lee looked for, but could not find, neither Wade nor Clarence, nor any of them.

"A thousand years may go by," he said, "and still the flavor of last night's meal will not have utterly been forgot."

"Books!" said Lulu. "Oh, I don't know. He used to be so…"

Lee shook with her. Her hand was thin and seemed to have too many little tiny bones in it. He saw where the hens had pecked at it, where fins had made it bleed, and where one nail had gone black. They'd not be seeing each other again—he knew it, she knew it, and the men knew it too, those who had gone off so as not to say it.

"Goodbye," said Lee.

"Well…"

Chapter Fifteen

THUS LEE, AND THUS LEE'S WIFE—THEY HAD COME DOWN INTO THAT ALABAMA STASIS IN WHICH THE DAYS HAD LOST THEIR NAMES AND RAN IN JUMBLED ORDER—SAVE ONLY FOR "FRIDAYS," WHEN, AFTER A WEEK OF STEADY DRINKING, HIS MIND TENDED TO FUZZ UP, AND HE COULD ALMOST SYMPATHIZE WITH ORDINARY PEOPLE.

Shortly after noon, he woke, rolled, groaned, drank, and then stumbled out into the sun. She was not in the house and not in the barn. Noiselessly, he crept down to the edge of the woods and stood listening. Someday—he knew it—she would come to him when he least expected it, would whisper something he could not understand, and then would turn and trudge away. Or, grow too small for him to find her. Sadly, he headed back for bed. That was when he heard, "Caw! Caw!" and realized that this time it was no real crow, but rather Judy herself using their secret code.

He plunged into the woods, but almost at once ground down to a halt when he saw the great number of natural objects that littered the forest—pine cones as big as his head and, here and there, a grey boulder with antique inscriptions that ran down into the earth. The history of these woods had never yet been written, nor, so far as he knew, had these engravings been touched by modern scholarship. Among it all, he counted four hundred beer cans (more or less), and at least two discarded refrigerators that he felt disinclined to open. The toadstools, the few that survived, were misshapen and looked like human glands. Yes, nature answered to the outside world, and was decaying with the towns. And yet, nothing could have prepared him for the plethora of advertisements and handbills posted everywhere, including one that seemed to be promoting that same management seminar that he had refused last month in New York. Moreover, in place of the usual Monday-night revivals that he remembered from childhood— instead of that he saw summons after summons to the regular Tuesday-night group-therapy circle, an invitation for the bean farmers to come into touch with their *authentic* feelings; he wanted to puke. Here where formerly there had been his grandmother's bee glade, now someone had tossed away a half-eaten lunch with pizza crusts, two beer cans, and a disposable needle. He wanted to weep, to vomit, to run and fetch his pistol; instead, that minute, he heard the unmistakable sound of a bell, a blithe one that seemed to be coming toward him from a few degrees off toward the west.

Lee hid. The woman, she was very definitely moving straight toward him, and very definitely indeed, as was her wont, carrying on a dark conversation with her soul. She looked good to him, especially so in woods. And now, having viewed her, he wanted to lie with her at once.

"Oh!" (She leapt back.) "I didn't know you were here."

"I intended it that way."

"Have you had your morning coffee?" (She actually began to move toward the house, presumably to prepare the coffee.)

"Hold!" said Lee. "What do you have there?"

"Plums! Want one?"

"They're scuppernongs."

"No, plums. Want one?"

He plopped the thing into his mouth. *Now* it all came flooding back—the uncanny taste that derived only from his own land alone. He had set aside one certain cell in his head for just this memory and no other.

"Yes, it's good; I admit it."

"I know! Want another?"

But this one was not nearly so good. In the '40s, he had been able to consume thirty of them before hitting upon one that was bitter. Again, the "bell" sounded. Incredibly, she had rigged up a collar for Glam II, using red ribbon for string and the two apartment keys from New York to make the chime.

"Shall we go back to the house now, you and I?"

"For the coffee?"

Lee said nothing. She was small and possibly getting smaller, but remained astonishingly heavy for her size and weight. He assisted her across the creek. Her brown hair, it had faded somewhat to be sure, but only to the extent that it now sorted perfectly with the color of the woods. And now, once more, he had her in his arms and his nose in her hair; she could not get away. Of course, she was herself so much like the woods and fields, fields, woods, flowers, and rue, this craving would never end.

Chapter Sixteen

Y EARS DID PASS, OR RATHER A FEW DAYS IN WHICH THEIR ADAPTATION
TO THINGS WAS THAT OF YEARS. Thus, one afternoon, he found
himself in the barn putting together a few odds and ends of
furniture out of the stuff at hand. He admired good workmanship; his own skill, however, had abandoned him. First,
he constructed a bookcase, an unsteady affair that might
almost have been tacked together by a child.

Of books themselves—and he had numbers of them—
he took one now, permitting it to fall open where it would,
and to lie unresistingly in his hand. Yes, it was Sweet's
Anglo-Saxon Grammar, the sheer oddity of the language
making him believe at first that he had forgotten how to
read! Next, he had two brown tomes smeared on fore-edge
with dust and gold, also a lovely green book the color of
celery that was like unto a bright and cheerful day when
grass grows high around a lake. The following volume
cheered him even more—a "fat man" with ruddy cheeks
and some of the original jolly jacket still adhering to the
spine. Lee had preserved it for its looks alone and never
for its contents, which he could not abide. Finally, hand
trembling, he came down to his two very different versions
of Homer, each better than the other, but neither better
than Murray's, the best translation of them all. Right away,
he put the first of them away in the cabinet, and the other

next to the first. Now, standing back, he smoked. Murray he put in his vest.

And all during this while, the sun outside was so bright that it seemed to give off a hum. He noted it when a cat came out of hiding and then proceeded halfway across the open space between house and barn before stopping suddenly and then racing back in great distaste. This *was* that two-hour period of each day in Alabama when time slowed and almost stopped, and when no one in right mind would choose to be outside. The window itself had a film over it, rendering one pane opaque even while the other granted a far-off picture of smoke and hills and two carmine barns. This then was how he expected to await the twenty-first century—with woman and books, and with painterly scenes to take the breath away. No more journeying! He was finished with it.

Chapter Seventeen

It RAINED THAT NIGHT AGAIN—HE COULD SCARCE BELIEVE IN HIS GOOD FORTUNE. Judy, meanwhile, was contending with the stove, a great black item that had not been in operation during the whole post-historical period. Night was closing in, a far more portentous operation than in the city. Here, it brought a sense of fright.

They made a meal of beans, bacon, cheese, and brandy, all of it topped off with a sweet farkleberry wine. They ate quietly however, so as not to give away their location. Suddenly, outside, the gigantic forest fell silent too, as if the crickets had all been singing from the same score. Something thudded down on the roof and then flew away; clearly, the creatures were slaughtering one another outside, even as much as in the city. Finally he pushed back and went to the window, but only to discover his own face peering back in the pane.

"Think then of this, wife, namely that whereas we might be here, a home with holes in it, yet those others, those in the cities where the late twentieth century…" He stopped. She couldn't hear, not with the crickets having picked up again with their shrieks and screams. Instead, he went to the desk and pulled his books and papers up around him. He had much to do, and very little fuel left in the paraffin lamp. His wife had finished in the kitchen and had gone upstairs; now she reappeared in a nineteenth-century garb taken from one of the trunks.

"Poor baby," she said, laying a hand on his shoulder. "You work so hard. What are you making?"

"It's a blueprint."

"Of your roasting machine?"

He nodded. "I'm adding a second entrance to it. One for the rich people, and the other…"

"For the Philistines?"

"Right."

He worked until past midnight and then, having slumbered off on the couch, woke and drank. The rain was languishing. There was still enough of it, however, to go on dripping all night, in the way he adored.

Taking the revolver, he stepped out onto the porch. The sky was gorgeous, and made more gorgeous by the bright green rings of pollution hanging over Birmingham. It was the moon that was deleterious, a lump of consolidated semen squeezed between the clouds. Two stars only were visible— Hector and Andromache circling around each other forever in synchrony. Now, half-drunk, he began what was to become a routine with him, namely that of shutting his eyes and concentrating, and then of calling down upon the outside world his whole inventory of curses and fates and new diseases, until at length it soothed him, and he could withdraw back inside.

His wife lay in the innermost chamber, her eyes wide open as she stared up in wonder from her cot. After thirty years, they communicated with eye beams alone.

"Shall I put thee to sleep now dear?"

She nodded, whereupon he lifted and turned her, and then began kneading her about the shoulders and spine. It needed ten seconds, no more, before she whimpered once and fell unconscious. Finally, he summoned the dog to come and watch over her for the next seven hours, until such time as she might wake again, just as she had done every morning of her life, with tremendous aplomb.

"And are you well asleep now dear?"

She nodded with enthusiasm. Outside, the moon had changed again and seemed now to have ants on it or, possibly, automobiles.

He went out and headed for the woods, but then changed his mind and aimed for the car. What surprised him was not that the radio was full of babbling and yowling—he expected that—but rather that there was actually some good music coming in from Birmingham. He dithered with the dial, turning slowly through the static and through tides of ignorance, breaking through space and time. Housing starts were down and, worse still, some of September's projects had been postponed. Next, he learned, troops were being sent forward to Asia, Africa, and/or Latin America. He turned back, almost running past the Berlioz *Requiem* that now was coming in rather more tenuously than at the first. Good music, and at a time in history when not one soul could have been found that was good enough to serve as Berlioz's plumber's whore. This then was how the last good people ought to communicate—by way of books and music, over the miles and over the years, meeting never.

He closed and locked the car, and then stepped to the back of the house. No possible doubt, there *was* certainly a community thriving in the bottoms—he could hear the resonant coffee-colored voices that seemed to well up out of the valley. He listened for it, bending into the hickory smoke lifting from the chimneys down below. Cold weather was coming nearer; it made him want to rush in to his wife and to sleep for ten thousand years in her arms. Instead, he crossed over to the barn.

Here too the roof had largely blown away, allowing starlight in. Somehow he had still imagined the place to be under the keeping of the great mule that had so lorded it over the others, before toiling himself to death in the corn. There had been personalities in those days, the space was haunted by them. Lee squeezed into one of the compartments, a comfy cell that had still the smell and perhaps even some of the original heat of the creature that had tenanted there once.

These extinct ones, they had transmogrified into pure spirit during his long absence, and now he was able to get into the same booth with them with no unseemly jostling, nor fear of getting nipped.

He went back to the car and again tried the radio. This time, rioting had broken out in St. Louis and (although they seemed reluctant to report it) the police had been withdrawn. Durables were down. Now again, just as they were about to give the weather, static interrupted; he saw the tiny bulb flicker, die, come back on again. (Always he looked upon weather as prescient of what was likely to happen next in history; now all he could hear was something about rain in Tennessee.) And meanwhile a soprano was striving mightily to break in with a message about a certain brand of dental floss.

He returned to the shelter of the porch. The stars, mutating wildly during the past half-hour, now differed hugely in both brilliance and size. Lee smoked, setting off the crow, or grackle, or whatever it was that had followed all the way from Maryland. Even here, even now, the thing would *not* leave off jibing at him.

He went in. His wife, she had always been rather small, and at night she seemed to draw up even more. He came closer. It was a good woman, the world's best, and never mind all his own personal philosophic trash that he had tried to fob off onto her. It was the dog that wouldn't let him come closer. Three times he tried before giving it up and going for one of the candles, and taking it outside.

Halfway to the woods, he trod upon something, a doll of some sort that had been made from straw. Lee got down and looked at it bemusedly, calm enough at first, until he realized that the thing (it wore a little set of dark glasses made from wire) had been designed to look like…himself! Worse still, a long-handled knitting needle had been driven through the heart of it. Lee jumped back, exclaiming out loud. His best job now would have been to return to the house at once and to lock himself in with his wife; instead, he continued forward.

Chapter Eighteen

BUT HAD NOT GONE FAR BEFORE HE BEGAN TO HAVE AN AESTHETIC EXPERIENCE. This dazzling night (already it filled the valley) had been conjured by one of the Negroes down below who was so old and so tired, apparently he had forgot to leave off conjuring before he slept. And now Lee must find and awaken him, and soon, too, or else this dazzling night might overflow the earth!

Lee therefore hurried down into the valley, calling for the man and drinking on the run. The "settlement," when he came to it… In truth, it was not so much a settlement as simply two shacks constructed randomly out of boards and sheets of advertising signs. Lee must be inordinately careful here—already two small but garrulous-looking dogs had caught whiff of him and had begun to moan. That these shacks did have people in them, he could infer it from the smoke lifting from both pebble-made chimneys, from the car out front, and from the light in one of the windows.

It angered him that they felt so free about making use of land that in theory belonged to him alone, a feeling that they had felt for fifty years and more. It angered him too that there were at least another half-dozen such communities that had grown up over the years, forming, as it were, a *cordon africain* between himself and the outside world. Yes, he could put a match to it, but what good would it do? Six months thereafter and there'd be green corn growing in the ashes.

Lee came nearer, holding the candle high. The dogs, at least, *they* were willing to acknowledge whose land it was—it charmed him to have them sniffing at his shoes and sniffing at his pockets, refusing to bark. And when he looked into the window itself, finding there a conjurer in inch-thick glasses who was reading late, late into the night in a book that was thick, very thick, and with an opened jeweled cask in which, apparently, the book was normally stored...Lee was charmed even more.

He came away. It was in this precinct that some of his noblest and most ancient pines were to be found, hundred-year-old incarnations tortured horribly by sun and fire, and by the periodic gales that came even this far sometimes from the Gulf of Mexico. To west was waste, a full thirty acres of barren land where—nothing surprised him anymore (he had come to expect *anything*)—where millions of the local "land crabs" had emerged to bathe themselves one last time in the mellow moon before winter arrived. He stepped with great care; the things had carapaces that were thick but brittle, and that gave off a sharp retort whenever they were trod upon. In any case, he was drawing nigh to the boundary that divided him off from the unfriendly farmer who held the adjoining acres.

He moved on hurriedly, drinking on the run. A briar caught hold of his tie and pulled it out, whereupon, after wasting two minutes with it, he took out the pistol and blasted himself free. In the silence that followed, he heard a distant rooster bawling out loudly, hours ahead of schedule. No doubt about it, there was quite as much life and striving, just as much "Will to Power" in the night as ever by day. Night, however, entailed more *fear*. He hummed, drank, whistled; for the past minutes he had been pulled on by what at first he believed to be an old opera tune playing in his head; now, he saw in fact that the music was proceeding from a certain point perhaps three hundred yards off in the direction of the river. This *was* disconcerting—no one had been conceded the right to produce music in what was his own favorite location in all the world.

He sprinted toward it, cursing. He had come to Alabama to be shut of people, not to discover each day new neighbors on land that was supposed to be his own. Now not only had this trespasser trespassed, but he had also helped himself to some very fine timbers in building his home. But what infuriated Lee, what set him to cursing and loading his gun, was how the cabin was sitting out so blatantly in the open, where he ought long before to have noticed it, each time he looked across the field.

And yet… He could not fail to appreciate the construction, the neatness of it, the "plumb-and-socket" joinings and stained-glass windows. The room itself, however, although lit up brightly, was empty. Gun in hand, Lee raced around to the other side. Here he had to fight to get a view, finally dangling, as it were, from the overhang of the roof, in order to see inside.

Nothing surprised him anymore—the man continued to play on his cello while at the same time smiling back at Lee cordially, even nodding with his head to beckon him inside.

"Kodály!" Lee yelled. Then: "This is *my* land, *mine!*"

The man smiled. He did not, however, come to the door until the piece was finished.

"Mine, mine, mine!"

"Anything you'd like to hear?"

"You should know that I have a pistol too!"

It was a medium-sized person, largely bald and conservatively dressed. Lee was flabbergasted to see that the man had a book collection very nearly as extensive as his own. He went on:

"You've got your cheek! Squatting just here where I ought to have noticed you long ago."

"Ah. But you see, I agree with Hooker."

"Hooker?" Lee came closer. In the cabin, he did not really need the candle anymore.

"Yes, yes, Hooker." (For a moment, Lee thought he was about to go back to sawing on his instrument.) "That to be *truly* obscure, it is best to be out in the open about it. To wit: you knew about the Negroes long before you knew about me."

It was true. Lee sank down slowly in the nearest chair. He was tired, it was late, the cabin was well made. "*My* land!" he said again, though his heart wasn't in it.

"Anything you'd like to hear?"

"I wouldn't mind the Kodály again. Hold! First a cup of hot coffee please, well sweetened."

The man started to go off for it, but then slowed, stopped, thought, and then came back to take the instrument with him. It gave Lee the chance, tired as he was, to rush up to the cabinet and take two conveniently sized paperback books, which he squirreled away in his vest. Some minutes went by. The cabin was so comfy and he so close to snoozing off… At last he was served with that which he had asked for.

"Very well! And now I'll hear the Kodály again."

"No, sorry; no, the mood has passed."

"I see. And so we sit here, you and I. And just what manner of cellist are you that you must be in proper 'mood' at all times?" (He could feel his gorge rising.)

"What manner?"

"Yes."

"Because *your* land—if it *is* yours… Well, you must understand that everyone considers you to have been dead for years."

"I see! And so why did you not then simply occupy the existing house, ha? Hm?" Lee grinned maliciously at him.

"The world's premier cellist, *that's* what manner."

"'Premier.' And how, pray, came you to be so grand?"

"What! And live in the same house with Pinky, the furniture all covered in fish scales?"

Lee felt tired. "Perhaps if I asked the same question twice…"

"It was the Deity made me so."

"Deity."

"Or One just like Him. See how frank I am?"

"The Deity made of you the grandest cellist on earth—no, I want to understand this."

"History."

"What?"

"Grandest in history."

"Ah. Now this Deity…"

"Or One just like Him."

"…appeared before you one day and…"

"Night."

"What?"

"He comes at night."

"Perhaps if *you* told the story…"

In fact, the man was on the point of refusing. Lee, however, rose slightly and pointed about at the surrounding land that was technically his. He was tired, and yet not so very tired that he couldn't listen. He drank. The room, as he now realized, held not books alone; it held also two straw dolls with little brown bottles in their hands. Outside, the crickets were making very little interference. Came now the story:

Chapter Nineteen

"**I** WAS ONLY FIVE," HE SAID, "OR ANYWAY CERTAINLY UNDER SEVEN. IT WAS A TIME WHEN PEOPLE LIKE YOU WERE FRITTERING AWAY THEIR YOUTH IN GAMES AND RADIO PROGRAMS, AND POTTERING AROUND IN THE OUT-OF-DOORS."

"Possibly."

"But I meanwhile, *I* was already two years into the violin."

"Two!"

The man fell into reverie. Lee waited for him.

"Yes. It came while I was sleeping—we lived in Ohio then— a peculiar rattling noise from the closet. Imagine my terror! I was only five. Great grinning Thing, clown-like in every respect, and me not yet seven. How would *you* like it? And that was when this...*comedian* (I speak figuratively of course) stepped up to the head of my small bed and stood grinning down upon a poor terrified wight who lay crying and calling and wanting nothing better than just to fall back to sleep again."

"The hound."

"Wearing a yellow tie, if I remember rightly. Picture of a girl on it in a bathing suit."

Lee's mind raced back through everything he had read in the Hindu scriptures concerning the apparel of the myriad gods. "*Yellow*, you say."

"'Play!' He said. 'Play for me something on your tiny guitar!'"

"Did you? Did you do it?"

"Oh now I understand—it's your land, and so you feel entirely free to interrupt me anytime you want."

Lee blushed.

"'Play for me something on your tiny guitar!' Well, you can just imagine my mortification. Fortunately, I kept the thing under my tiny bed. And what do you suppose He wanted to hear?"

Lee started to answer, but hushed when the man held up his finger to warn against it.

"Picture it! Pathetic little six-year-old trembling in his tiny pajamas with the little bears on them." (He was near to tears.) "'Play! Play! Else I'll nip off your little head!'—*that's* how He spoke to me."

"Bounder."

"And play I did. O how I did play! Playing and crying, crying and playing. The mortification of it, to see that He was laughing the whole while."

"Nothing surprises me. Not anymore."

"'No good!' He said. 'No good whatsoever. Why, you have no talent at all, none!' I cried, of course."

"I should think so."

"'No good! However, you *are* a good sport. Yes,' (He said), 'a very, *very* good sport.' (I who had never wanted aught to do with violins in the first place.) 'Therefore,' (He went on), 'I give you this, namely that you shall become the head guitar player of all time. I'm serious! The best of that whole crowd!' Well, you can just imagine. I thanked Him most devoutly, to be sure. And then He said this: 'But don't ask for *recognition*, oh no. No, that would be too much. Quality? Total quality. Recognition? None whatsoever. Now! Play for Me a sad tune on your tiny guitar.'"

Lee reeled. "You…"

"Exactly. Quality *and* recognition—that's what I wanted. I was only five!"

"But…"

"If you could just kindly shut up for two more minutes. Can you? Yes, I craved acknowledgment, I admit that. To go with the greatness of my playing."

"He craved it, yet was only five."

"And so I asked straight out: 'Couldn't I have both?' He laughed, of course."

"Thought He would."

"So there you have it. And now it should be clear to you, how I drifted down from one rotten little organization to the next—Billings Symphony Orchestra indeed!—my career languishing even as I myself went from good to great to better."

"Bloody hell! It must be even worse for a writer."

"Year after year after year—getting better and better!—after year after year after…"

"Hold! After all, you could have chosen the fame, no? And left quality alone."

"That's your idea of sportsmanship, is it?"

"Hold!" said Lee again. "At all events, at least you know better now than to go running after a secular success. And that, after all, is freedom of a sort."

The man grinned diabolically. "Would it were! No, you see it's quite possible that I dreamt it all. I was only five."

"And so…"

"Yes?"

"And so you can't be absolutely positive that…"

"Go on."

"That…"

"That I have even the quality! Hee! Ha! Ohhhh."

"Jesus! Why, you must be the most miserable man on earth. Year after year after… Oh! Oh! Oh! I don't envy *you*."

Far away, the rooster crowed again, this time only minutes too early. Lee drank. Night was ending, and he with five hundred yards that must be crossed soon, unless he wanted to risk it in broad daylight. It did please him that the man had taken up his cello again and was playing sweetly, a sublime piece from God's own favorite virtuoso.

Chapter Twenty

ON THE TWENTIETH DAY, HE WOKE TO A CHILL AND THE SOUND OF WOLVES IN THE HILLS. Overnight, the leaves had turned to umber, some of them finding a way into the house.

He drank and then, dressed in his pajamas still, drifted down into the lower field. He spied an antique harrow lying precisely where someone, caught by surprise when the epoch ended, had run off and left it. Here it was near to December, and the sun doing the very best that it could, with veins standing out on its face. And smells, such smells—it was not just grapes and not just fennel; the hills were reeking. It was owing to just such a burden of smells as these that his wife had twice discovered him listing in the field, both eyelids fluttering dangerously.

Manifestly, civilization here had fallen quite as much into decay as in the cities. And meanwhile the sky itself was long, high, far, short, narrow, and languourous to a degree; he saw one especially listless cloud that would wander no further. Himself, he was being drawn on toward the disused well that his people had excavated in old times, a sacred place with vines and gourds, and with some of the original stone-work yet remaining. And when he opened and looked down into the shaft, immediately he descried a fund of dark blue "ink" in which two gars were trying desperately to hide behind each other. The vines, the moss, they formed a superior sleeping place where at first he thought he might actually be able to doze off again, that is to say until he was joined by an elaborate insect in a lilac gown and four water-colored wings that made a sound like unto a beating heart. Indeed, he was continually amazed at things. *Here* were leaves like ancient manuscript, and *there* an abundance of blooms shaped like little waxen pots with powder on them. He knew this much, that back in the cities they would be *slicing* each other by now, *chewing*, *sucking*, *envying*, and going to cocktail parties. Thinking of it, he glowed with malice for a long time. Finally, he did stand and toss down the cigarette to the gar that had been waiting confidently for it all these years.

He hit the woods, drinking and bumbling his way down to the creek, where he frightened up a small brown bear supping at the water. It was all pines here, although the needles were not much more than half their length of former times. A thin red snake, too tiny to be feared, reared indignantly at first, but then changed its mind and whisked off through the grass as fast as it could go. Three times he called (Caw! Caw!) getting no answer. He had lost all direction, of course, and was simply following the bear.

The pond, when he came to it, was slime-covered and rather more greenish than he liked to see. He drank, wine *and* water, and then began making up a sleeping place out of pine needles. It dizzied him, watching the crazed water bugs skating back and forth insanely on their narrow feet. More worrisome still was the scarlet mite chasing across his knee; quickly, he changed into the more powerful of his two sets of glasses and tried to get a nearer look into what proved to be such a ferocious little face that he was sorry to have come to know about it. The dog, the dog was bored. It had been a long while since the passing of the great age of dogs, all the way down to this grinning example with loose lips and mind benumbed. Lee spun, focusing on him with eyes that had seen the beauty and the wisdom in five thousand books. At once, the dog began to blink and to water; nor did Lee stop with his glaring until he had forced the creature all the way home.

Lee smoked, thinking deeply. Someday—he had no doubt of this—the authorities would find him quite putrefied beneath a foot-deep covering of pine straw, his eyes still bulging wildly at the open book held up where the sun could hit it. Today, it was Thucydides he was reading, his fourth-, or sometimes fifth-favorite among the greater Greeks. Not to say that he had brought his favorite edition of it into the woods—far from it! He kept all such things as that locked up with the pistol and the brandy, and with all that share of the money that he had not already in wily shrewdness hidden on lands that were not really his. No, this was a cheap edition he was using today, cheap enough indeed that he had not objected to paying for it. And then, too, should he fall asleep, as he hoped that he would, and if he slobbered on it, as usually he did… "I'm getting old," he said. "And more hours than I like to think about before all falls dark once more."

Chapter Twenty-one

DAYS PASSED, OR RATHER WEEKS DURING WHICH HIS DETERIORATION WAS THAT OF DAYS ONLY. Winter came, stopped, went forward; nor was his wife growing any smaller.

One day, having been rooting about in the basement, he happened upon an old-fashioned photograph album that was only in part ruined by the moisture. He flew upstairs with it and then, talking to himself with excitement, went outside to sit upon the field and examine the thing in full light. The day, however, was gloomy, sad beyond belief; he saw one thin tendril of smoke lifting from the violinist's house. It wasn't true that "nothing surprised him anymore"; in fact, he was greatly and constantly surprised by the numbers of black people, entire nations as it seemed, migrating across his fields with luggage and cattle, their eyes fixed upon the seeming promise of Georgia's western hills.

He drank, and then suddenly opened the album wide. He saw first a child, the overexposed face of a last-century child. There was much fog in those days, or else the photographic chemical had itself turned unduly cloudy. By this time, the boy would be dead of old age, no doubt about that, but as to whether he had married or not, or whether participated in happiness to any extent... Lee came nearer. He had intended to look for the family features; instead, he found himself gazing deep, deep into the worried eyes of a soul which had never wanted to come into life in the first place. Lee came nearer still, taking off his glasses and *entering*, as it were, into the awful experience of having been new and small, and condemned to a life of farming. Lee wished him well, forgetting that the boy had already finished with all that long ago, and long ago had taken up his own special niche among the stars.

The next page showed the very house itself, and the very window in which someone seemed to be sitting in the dark. Suddenly, pointing, Lee exclaimed out loud—there was a woman, a shy one, a woman peeping around the corner of the house; Lee could see one shy eye. In *those* days, the structure had been hale and newly painted, and had a proud tin rooster sitting in noble profile athwart the gable. Quickly he went on to the following page where three soiled men were standing shoulder to shoulder and looking back frankly at the camera out of the dead, grey, extinct eyes of nineteenth-century farmers. *These* were his people, farmers and mail carriers and the like who, starting from nothing, had not only brought off an Age of Integrity, but had thought to take pictures of it as well.

Next, a cow, a very good one apparently—she had ribbons to her credit and a mirthful eye. Yes, it had been an epoch of extraordinary ambitions, he could read it both in their faces and in the peculiarly grainy texture of the light itself. All his hatred rolled away. Here, in pictures like these, every human error was redeemed, and more than redeemed, by the exercise of hardness and lovely gorgeous poverty. He saw next a woman in a bonnet who, in her embarrassment, had tried to hide her two vast hands. His excitement increased; he saw his own grandfather (Lee had only the slightest remembrance of him), a melancholy man who had eschewed all pleasure owing to the enormous amount of work that had to be done. The facing page showed his funeral, with people standing about in formal dress.

Lee moved on, crashing into modern times. There was a house—he remembered it—and then, with the integrity going out and color photography coming in, a picture of himself at age five standing in a child's version of a World War II uniform. Two pages further he could make out homes with the first television antennae on them, someone having bravely snapped a picture at the very instant when the country began to turn to slop.

It was all too much, too strange, the field too unsteady. He called twice, uselessly (where was she?), and then, holding the album high, drank twice, and crawled across the field.

Chapter Twenty-two

HE DID NOT ADMIT THAT IT WAS WINTER, NOT UNTIL THAT DAY THE SNOW CAME INTO THE ROOM WHERE HE WAS READING STUBBORNLY IN TWO SWEATERS AND HIS GRANDFATHER'S COAT. Snow. He cursed, stood, railed against it, but then did have finally to confess that such weather very often did bring with it a larger number of aesthetic experiences than mere summer and spring. Suddenly, spying a likely-looking volume in his case (dark blue and yellow cover on it), he stepped over with great subtlety (looking behind him) and hid it in his coat.

"Ah me," he said, "my chapters are getting shorter and winter now is here." Nothing surprised him anymore, and when he got to the porch, Judy was hurrying past, stick in hand, driving her ducks to the safety of the barn. It mortified him—glad was he that no one could see it—how she had fitted each of the little nuisances with a bright red jacket of its own. The dog! In weather like this, perfect for metabolism, his face looked precisely like a certain joyous Halloween mask that Lee remembered from his childhood years.

He tried it again in the afternoon, again stepping out onto the porch. This time, the hills were purple. No question about it, he had an experience coming on, and very little time in which to prepare. The woman meanwhile had restored the smokehouse to its former use—it was always her, *her* doing, *her* effort, *her* habit of tumbling out of bed at an early hour and then at an early hour tumbling back in, there to sleep full seven hours in honey and ambergris. Himself, he was indolent, had been so always; *his* job was experiences.

The sun, its confidence all gone, was blinking erratically as he climbed the hill. Lately he had taken to using a staff, doing it partly for the effect it had, but also in part as a weapon against the crows. Long ago he had learned the proper way to view landscapes, namely by looking *through* them, and *into* that elite domain where Time, Space, etc., had no sway. What he saw now was a blind swirl set with little cottages here and there. It would never fail to confuse him, how that the people could be as he knew them to be, while the cottages they built could be as nostalgically affecting as they were—it was a mystery. He cherished the small people, asking only that they stay off his land, or even a little further. That was when he descried six suede cows munching on weeds that were *definitely* his own, five of them sporting udders that were more than merely full.

He went higher. In his imagination, he almost expected to see The End of the West in some tangible form, as if it might come, when it did come, like a weather condition; instead, what he saw was an incipient "goat-based" culture rising in the east where until recently the uncomprehending farmers had been striving to make indigo crops in the alluvial chert. Now he saw something to make him reel—a peasant in a red blouse doing his plowing *now*, and using neither mules nor oxen nor machinery, but rather his own two stalwart sons.

Lee's mind flashed back to the centuries he had read about. This, mixed with the sound of an expert cello floating in and out of hearing, and mixed too with a dozen thin strings of smoke wending heavenward, and knowing too that in due course he was soon to know nothing, no, nor think anymore... He groaned, very loudly. The world indeed was yellow, burnt, highly detailed, and beset with calico mules.

Just then, one of the barns failed at last, collapsing in upon itself with almost no sound. History had come to a complete stop; he doubted whether it would ever start up again. And then, finally, he was allowed to see that for which he had come down south in the first place—his tiny wife. Saw her step out cautiously from the barn, saw her look about in all directions, saw her then join hands with the pig, the ducks, the dog, and saw them all go dancing in a circle. He put it down as one of his best experiences ever.

Chapter Twenty-three

T HAT VERY DAY, FOLLOWING THE ONE BEFORE, LEE ROSE EARLY AND, HUMMING, WENT FORTH TO THE END OF THE LANE AND FELLED THE SEVEN GREAT PINES, EFFECTIVELY SEALING THE PATH FOREVER.

"Ah yes," he said, speaking to himself. "Henceforth I study only Judy, books, the sun." He then went on: "And as for the outside world, may they all... And may they do it soon too!"

"But is there nothing you'll regret from beyond the seven pines?" (In fact, she was silent. Lee knew what she was thinking however.)

It was cold that night, a few wan stars trembling violently to keep warm. Lee nodded. The fire had burned down to a mess of ashes that seemed to give off voices (they were using seventy-year-old wood), and old familiar faces. Just then an animal, a fox or deer, stepped onto the porch, but didn't stay.

Such was his facility for reading, sometimes he was able to shut both eyes and go on without benefit of book. Already, three times, Judy had come to look in upon him, hungering for her evening walk.

"Now?" she asked. She was wearing mittens and a hat of some sort that made her look like a seal. Dressed so, he couldn't really say whether she was continually getting shorter or not.

It was grim night outside, veritably a jar of black, black ink. They stepped down cautiously into it, and then walked to the edge of the gorge.

"Hear that?" he asked.

No. Apparently the people had moved deeper; he could barely hear it himself. And then, too, the old folks had taken fright from the influx of charismatic flagellants coming down in droves from Tennessee. Lee told nothing of this to his wife. Furthermore, he had been trying for three nights to prevent her from seeing the new comet that had recently made its appearance over Alabama's skies, a green smear with a bifurcated tail, boding great bale for the county. Suddenly, the dog ran up, or part of him rather. For at night, he had a way of sticking his pastel face in and out of some other dimension. His voice, meanwhile, had turned to fog and came to them as through many fat layers of cloth.

"Comes now the barn," said Lee, "there, twenty yards in front. See? There where Aunt Betty had her creamery."

They passed on tiptoes, Lee making no mention of the two dozen straw dolls he had picked up in various places and hidden away in the loft. Ahead, the field was long, dark, creased, and so compacted by migrating Negroes that nothing would grow again. He didn't care. Nature was decaying; indeed, he could see balls of the stuff breaking off the upper hills and then tumbling as slowly as cotton into the gorge. The house itself, previously symmetrical, it too had melted into a running stream of tint. Something *was* happening; he had known it from the start.

"How much longer, Lee?"

"I don't know. I have still some four, or maybe five experiences. Six, including this one."

"Six." She thought. It seemed to satisfy her.

Tito Perdue
*was born in Chile in 1938. His
family returned to the United
States at the outbreak of war.
He received a B.A. in English
literature from the University of
Texas, and an M.A. in European
history and an M.L.S. from
Indiana University.
He has worked as a bookkeeper, an
apprentice insurance underwriter,
and a library administrator in the
Midwest and the North. In 1982,
he returned to the South and to
full-time writing.
THE NEW AUSTERITIES
is the prequel to his first novel,
LEE, which was published by
Four Walls Eight Windows in
1991. Perdue lives in
Cave Spring, Georgia,
with his wife, Judy.*